STEELDUST

BY

KEN FARMER

STEELDUST

BY
KEN FARMER

Cover Design by: Mike Beckom
and Ken Farmer
Cover Model: Emma Lou Cunningham

THE AUTHOR

Ken Farmer didn't write his first full novel until he was sixty-nine years of age. He often wonders what the hell took him so long. At age seventy-six...he's currently working on novel number twenty-two.

Ken spent thirty years raising cattle and quarter horses in Texas and forty-five years as a professional actor (after a stint in the Marine Corps). Those years gave him a background for storytelling...or as he has been known to say, "I've always been a bit of a bull---t artist, so writing novels kind of came naturally once it occurred to me I could put my stories down on paper."

Ken's writing style has been likened to a combination of Louis L'Amour and Terry C. Johnston with an occasional Hitchcockian twist...now that's a combination.

In addition to his love for writing fiction, he likes to teach acting, voice-over and writing workshops. His favorite expression is: "Just tell the damn story."

Writing has become Ken's second life: he has been a Marine, played collegiate football, been a Texas wildcatter, cattle and horse rancher, professional film and TV actor and now...a novelist. Who knew?

Web page: www.KenFarmer-Author.net

ACKNOWLEDGMENT

The author gratefully acknowledges T.C. Miller and Lt. Colonel Clyde DeLoach, USMC (Ret.) for their invaluable help in proofing and editing this novel.

ISBN-13: - 978-0-9984703-9-9 Paper
ISBN-10: - 0-9984703-9-2
Timber Creek Press
Imprint of Timber Creek Productions, LLC
312 N. Commerce St.
Gainesville, Texas 76240

Published by: Timber Creek Press
timbercreekpresss@yahoo.com
www.timbercreekpress.net
Twitter: @pagact
Facebook Book Page:
www.facebook.com/TimberCreekPress
Ken's email: pagact@yahoo.com
214-533-4964

DEDICATION

Steeldust is dedicated to my son, Clayton Farmer. I couldn't be more proud of anyone than I am of him. I also dedicate this novel to my brothers and sisters in the United States Marine Corps. Oorah! Semper Fi.

TIMBER CREEK PRESS

CHAPTER ONE

PALO PINTO COUNTY, TEXAS

A bullet ricocheted from the large boulder and whined mournfully off into the distance. The boom of a long gun sounded a half-second later.

"Great jubilee," exclaimed Slim Parker as he, Lisanne Gifford, and Sheriff Mason Flynn flinched at the rock chips that peppered their faces and immediately took cover behind the boulder.

Ken Farmer

Lisanne's big yellow dog, Barney, took cover with them.

They regretfully watched a magnificent sixteen hand steeldust stallion squeal, spin on his heels and gallop off down into the coolie toward his herd of mares. His blue-gray metallic appearing hair showed a chatoyant shimmer in the morning light.

"Dang. Almost touched him," said Lisanne, leaning back against the rock.

"See where that shot come from, Slim?" asked Flynn.

"Cross the way yonder, Sheriff...least a quarter mile. Wind's too strong for the gunsmoke to stay put long. But, sounded like a big bore...not as big as my Sharps, but, big enough," said the skinny Chickasaw Freedman.

"Reckon they were shootin' at us or that stallion, Sheriff?" the seventeen year old cute blond asked.

"Take your pick, Lisanne. They're either a damn good shot an' hit exactly what they aimed at or a lousy one if they were shootin' at you or the horse."

"Hope it didn't spook that stallion none too bad. You done spent purtnear a hour talkin' to him an' gittin' him to let you walk almost up to him. You

2

gots a way with wild horses, girl...yessirrebob, a real way," said Slim.

"Well, I hope they were shootin' at me. Would hate to see anythin' happen to Steeldust," she said.

"That what you're gonna name him...Steeldust?" asked Flynn.

Lisanne nodded. "Just as well call him what he is...Name fits, don'tcha think?"

"Gotta agree with you there...Any idea who might have throwed that shot our way?" asked the sheriff as he looked around the edge of the boulder trying to see any movement across the draw.

"I do."

He looked back at her. "Well?"

"That pompous, pridefull bastard...sorry about the language, but that's what he is...that owns those ten sections between my place and Bryson...Thinks he owns everything and everybody in Jack County...includin' Steeldust." Lisanne rubbed her right eye trying to get the grit from the ricochet out.

"Oh, yeah. Algernon Sinclair, the III...and his three sons. Moved down here from Denver." Flynn chuckled. "Pride is a rooster crowin' on a cow pie...Had a couple of run-ins with him myself. Think he's somehow involved with a rustlin' ring,

3

but, can't get any evidence on him...What's he done to you?"

"He's tried to buy me out several times and now has resorted to out and out threats...Had a couple of mysterious grass fires recently."

"What kinda threats?" asked Flynn.

"Said it would be a shame if something happened to Barney or if my house caught fire...You know, bullyin' stuff."

"Reckon me an' my new bride might need to go have a chat with good ol' Algernon an' his brood...up close an' personal."

"I'd watch my back, Sheriff. He's got 'bout ten men a workin' fer 'im, not countin' them pups. None of 'em 're cowhands...They all gunhawks, you ask me," said Slim.

Flynn looked around the boulder. "I'd say whoever shot at us is gone...or they're gone."

"They?" asked Lisanne.

"Yep. Two dust trails headin' west...Let's slip over 'cross the arroyo an' see as they left anythin' stupid."

They climbed back up to the edge of the draw to their own mounts, cinched up, mounted and headed toward the other side.

STEELDUST

The trio dismounted on the west side of the gully and made their way down to the point they figured the shot came from.

"Uh, huh," said Slim. ".45-70 casin', 'bout like I figgered. Most likely a Winchester." He picked up the brass from the ground near the bottom of the boulder.

Flynn noticed some dark stains on the rock and the ground, and then picked up several quirly butts. "Here for a while...waitin' on us. One with a chaw an' the other smokin' Bull Durham."

"How can you tell it's Bull Durham?" asked Lisanne.

"It's a lighter color and not as strong as Prince Albert."

"You don't smoke cigarettes, how do you know?"

He glanced over at the seventeen year old. "My sweet wife told me an' she got it from Bass Reeves."

"Fair to middlin' source...My opinion," commented Slim. "They say he ain't never failed to bring in some miscreant once he been give paper on 'im."

"Been mor'n one that turned themselves in when they heard Bass was on their tail...startin' with Belle Starr," added Flynn.

"That's what a reputation kin do," said Slim.

"Reckon we oughta follow 'em?" asked Lisanne.

"No need. One thing I learned from Bass hisself was you don't always have to track some nabob...just go where they're goin'," said the sheriff. "I'd say let's go to my place. I mind Fiona'll have some dinner on the table time we get there."

"Hellova law, great cook an' right easy on the eyes...You got yerself a real keeper there, Sheriff," quipped Slim.

"I'd say," said Flynn, grinning, as he turned and hiked back up to where they had left their mounts.

"How long did it take you to teach that mustang mare to ground tie, Lisanne?" asked Flynn as he snugged the cinch on his blue roan Morgan, Laddie.

"'Bout two weeks." She stepped up into her double-rigged Texas style saddle. "Took most of it to teach her to just stand calm, tied at the corral or hitchrail by her lead an' leavin' her reins on the ground. Once she figured out she was supposed to stay where I put her when I left, wadn't any hill atall."

"Said she has a way with horses, didn't I," commented Slim. "That little girl talks to 'em an' the thing is, they seem to know what she's a sayin'."

"Durn…Took me a month to teach my Laddie," Flynn said.

Lisanne grinned and glanced over at him as they squeezed their mounts up into a medium trot through the scattered mesquite that was just starting to show early spring buds. "You just weren't holdin' your mouth right, Sheriff."

"Uh, huh." He looked over at Slim who also grinned and nodded at him.

"It'll take that kid another two weeks fer her to git that close to that stallion now," said Big Jim French. "Boss'll be tickled."

"Give us a chanct to lay a noose on that big sumbitch…Draggin' a railroad tie 'round fer a week er so will take some of the starch out." Fats McClure spat a long stream of brown tobacco juice in the direction of a horned toad on a rock as they loped by.

Ken Farmer

Big Jim looked over at his skinny-as-a-rail partner. "Easier said than done, Fats…easier said than done."

JACK COUNTY, TEXAS
BROKEN DIAMOND F RANCH

Flynn, Lisanne and Slim reined up at the front of the sheriff's ranch home almost at noontime.

Newton was prancing on the wraparound front porch as they stepped down, loosened their mount's cinches and tied up to the hitchrails.

Barney jumped up on the porch so he and Newton could trade rear end sniffs. Once the canine greeting ritual was satisfied, the pair laid down side by side on the porch to watch their humans.

Fiona Flynn, Mason's new bride and the only female Special Deputy US Marshal in the nation, opened the gingerbread screendoor and stepped out on the porch. The tall, raven-haired beauty was drying her hands on a dish towel.

She threw the towel aside, ran down the steps, jumped into Flynn's arms and covered his face with kisses. "Missed you."

"Dang! Think I'll stay gone longer than three hours next time."

Fiona leaned back. "You do, mister, and those kisses will become knots on your head."

"Yes, *Ma'am*." He grinned and tried to duck the slap to the back of his head for calling her 'Ma'am—her pet peeve.

He pecked her on the lips. "I love you."

"I love you, too...I suspect ya'll are hungry since you managed to get back here just as I had dinner ready...Anybody like chicken and dumplin's?"

"Yum. Thought you'd never ask," quipped Lisanne. "Just need to wash up."

"That goes for all of you. Think you have enough trail dust on you to start a garden...You know where the wash basin is. Bucket's full...I'll bring a couple more towels out."

Fiona nodded her head toward the wash stand at the east end of the porch with the white porcelain bucket hanging above it.

"Don't take all day...Got some cold Lone Star Beer, too...But not for you, young lady...Been keeping in down in the well...See to your horses first." She turned and went back inside.

Ken Farmer

"Hotdangomighty," Slim exclaimed. "Cold beer!"

BAR S RANCH

Big Jim French and Fats McClure drew rein in front of the large two-story native-stone ranch house with green shutters and a galvanized standing-seam metal roof. The three Sinclair boys were sitting on the porch with their after dinner coffee and smokes.

"How'd it go, Frenchy?" asked the oldest, Algernon, the fourth, who went by Al.

The two gunhands tied their mounts to the hitch rail out front and stepped up to the porch.

"Put the fear of God in that little split-tail…Shot right 'tween her an' that big stallion. She an' that bad assed sheriff an' her nigger hired-hand didn't waste no time duckin' fer cover…" He chuckled. "That cayuse lit a shuck back to his herd."

"Sheriff didn't shoot back?" asked Rowdy, the second oldest.

"Naw, they's too busy gittin' behind the rocks," answered Fats."

10

STEELDUST

"Damn shore save some trouble if ya'll had've just plugged the three of 'em," commented the hotheaded youngest, Carter.

"That ain't the way Pa wants to do it. You know how testy he can git we don't do what he says," said Al.

"Well, what he don't know don't hurt 'im none," replied Carter.

"What don't who know?" came a deep voice from the doorway.

§§§

CHAPTER TWO

JACK COUNTY, TEXAS
BROKEN DIAMOND F RANCH

"By the Lord Jim, Marshal, these is good dumplin's, uh, huh," said Slim as he put another spoonful in his mouth, closed his eyes in ecstasy, and then swallowed. "How is it you make 'em?"

Fiona smiled. "You know if I told you, Slim, I'd have to kill you."

Flynn snorted a little beer from his nose at the comment, and then wiped his dark mustache with his napkin. "She ain't funnin', pard. Don't share her recipes with nobody."

"But, you're welcome here anytime to share what I fix." She winked and smiled again.

Parker swallowed and nodded. "Uh, yes…" He stopped before he said 'Ma'am. "…Uh, Miz Flynn."

"And don't look at me, I can't make 'em either," commented Lisanne as she took another bite and dribbled some of the juice on her chin and denim shirt.

Fiona smiled. "My grandmother always said it was better if you wore some of it."

Lisanne grinned back in embarrassment and wiped her chin and shirt with her napkin.

"Just wait till ya'll have some of her dewberry cobbler for desert," said Mason.

The four started their after-dinner coffee when they finished the cobbler.

"Dang, if'n you wasn't right Sheriff," said Slim, as he patted his always trim stomach, and then looked at Fiona. "That was larripin' good, Marshal."

"Thank you, Slim, glad you enjoyed it…So, how's your mare herd coming along, Lisanne?" asked Fiona.

"Got five so far. Walt and Fran agreed to sell me three of their Standardbred long fillys in the spring…I'm really excited about that."

"They've got excellent stock," replied Fiona.

"'Specially if I can finally get Steeldust 'fore the Sinclairs do. I know how they catch wild horses…It's not pretty," said Lisanne as she pinched her lips.

She turned to Slim. "If you'll go get our horses, I'll help Fiona with the dishes."

"I kin do that, missy." He laid his napkin down and got to his feet.

"Give you a hand, Slim," said Flynn.

"You just want to get away from the dishes," commented Fiona.

He grinned at his wife. "Given the choice of doin' dishes or saddlin' mounts…reckon I'll pick tackin' ever time."

Fiona's steel-gray eyes sparkled as she got to her feet. "Maybe we'll save the pots and pans for you, husband."

"Oh, lordy…Think I'd rather be whipped with a wet rope."

She grinned and pecked him on the cheek. "That can be arranged, too."

He swatted her shapely behind, turned and followed Slim out the door, commenting over his shoulder, "Don't get kinky now, Missus Flynn."

She smiled coyly. "Shakespeare said, 'Flesh stays no further reason But rising at thy name'."

Mason turned with a frown on his face. "What?"

"Explain later…Now, scat."

Lisanne looked up at the taller woman after they closed the door behind them. "Do you mind if I ask you a question?"

Fiona smiled as she glanced back at the blonde seventeen year old. "Of course."

"What was the first thing that attracted you to Sheriff Flynn?"

She didn't have to pause. "He makes me laugh."

BAR S RANCH

The fifty-year old, barrel-chested, Algernon Sinclair, III, stood in the doorway, his arms folded across his chest and glaring at his youngest offspring. "Well?"

Carter looked down at his scuffed boots. "Nothin', Pa."

"Don't lie to me, boy."

"Uh…well, just said Frenchy and Fats shoulda just plugged the girl an' them others while they had the chance, Pa…That's all."

"Dammit, told you didn't want to do things that way…just yet. Killin' a Texas sheriff an' a young girl would bring the Rangers an' Federal Marshals down on us like stink on crap…You do what I tell you…Understand, Carter?"

"Yeah, Pa."

Algernon glared at his other sons and the two gunslingers. "Goes for the rest of you jackanapes, too…and I'm the last person on this planet you want to piss off…Trust me on that." He spun on his heel and headed back into the house mumbling, "Brains were dynamite, that bunch couldn't blow their noses."

"Gits a mite testy, don't he?" whispered Frenchy.

STEELDUST

Carter leaned forward in his chair, peeking over at the doorway before he spoke, "Yeah…But what I said still goes."

FLYING L RANCH

Lisanne and Slim trotted their horses through the gate to her horse ranch. Barney padded alongside of her four stocking, blaze-faced chestnut mare.

"I'll go out an' check on the stock, Miss Lisanne…See as we gots 'ny new babies on the ground 'fore I unload that wagon of hay the Sheriff and Fiona sent over."

"Be fine, Slim. Gotta check Sally's shoes. She's favorin' her right front some."

"Meby it's jest a rock in the frog groove."

"Maybe," she said as she dismounted at the front of the barn next to the water trough. "I'll cut some steaks off one of the hams in the smokehouse to go with the pinto beans I put on to slow cook before we left…Make some biscuits to go with that sorghum Miz Waverly brought over."

Ken Farmer

"Yum, yum...sounds good," Slim said over his shoulder as he nudged his gelding in the direction of the mare pasture.

Lisanne dismounted, jerked her saddle, pad and headstall, and then carried them into the tack room just inside the big double-hung doors.

She walked back out with the farrier's box, leaned over at the mare's right front and picked the hoof up. Sure enough, there was a pebble wedged in the groove between the sole and the frog.

The teenager pulled the hoof pick out of the box. Slim had made it for her from an old horseshoe by cutting the shoe in half, bending the top end over and grinding it down into a hook. It was ideal for cleaning out the groove without cutting the frog like a knife could do.

She popped the small rock free and cleaned both grooves before checking the tightness of the nails. Satisfied, she patted Sally on the neck, took a hog hair brush and gave her an appreciated brushing and combed out her mane and tail.

"You ready for your hay and a bait of grain, girl?"

The mare nodded her head and chuckled.

"All right, come on."

Lisanne walked into the wide alleyway and opened the door to Sally's stall. The mare followed behind her, stepped in, turned around at her feed bucket and waited patiently for her gallon of oats.

After her bucket was filled, Lisanne threw a block of prairie hay into the opposite corner. She grabbed a clean towel from the tack room, headed back out of the barn and toward the smokehouse.

She lifted the wooden latch to the plank door and pulled it open. Grabbing her Bowie from her belt, Lisanne stepped over to one of the hams hanging from the ceiling.

It had been smoked, along with other hams, shoulders, hog jowl, salt pork and sides of bacon from their last hog slaughter for three weeks over a slow mesquite charcoal fire.

She spun the ham around and gasped, "What in the…"

Almost half of the back side of the ham had been sliced away. She glanced over at the bacon sides—part of one of them was missing, too.

She sliced some more from the ham, muttering, "Got a damn thief 'round here…bet I catch 'em, whoever they are. Worked too hard raisin' an'

19

butcherin' them hogs for some yahoo to just come in here an' take what they want."

Wrapping the slices of ham in the towel, she stepped back outside, latched the door and carefully studied the ground.

"Well, that's interestin'." Lisanne knelt down and looked closely at the tracks leading away from the smokehouse toward the creek. "Barefoot."

§§§

CHAPTER THREE

PALO PINTO COUNTY, TEXAS
POSSUM KINGDOM LAKE, 2018

"You're gonna enjoy this, Pard, trust me."

Inspector Loraine Rodriguez, a beautiful Hispanic woman in her thirties, with an ample bosom, looked at inactive Force Recon Marine, 6'8" Detective Darrell Ulysses Bone of the Cross Police Department over the top of her sunglasses.

"Bone, anytime you say, 'trust me', I know to grab my butt, 'cause something bad is fixing to happen."

"You cut me to the quick, Pard. Would I ever lead you astray?...Don't answer that...Here."

He handed her the tackle box from his restored '73 Volkswagen Thing while he grabbed their rods and lunch box.

"We'll go down to that cliff that overlooks the lake. It's easy to cast out into the channel where the Brazos River used to run."

"When did they dam it up?"

Bone walked past her toward the shore of the seventeen thousand acre lake. "Ah...They started it in 1936 and completed in '41...There's some catfish in there bigger'n you."

"Get out of town."

"Kid you not, Pard. Padrino and I've scuba dived it several times...ran into some real monsters down there. The Brazos valley, under the water now, was chock full of caves an' hidin' places...They say the Comanche an' later outlaws, includin' Sam Bass, hid out here...We shoulda brought sleepin' bags and camped out."

"Told you the closest I'll go to camping out is a Holiday Inn."

"Wusse."

"You don't have to squat in the bushes with the bugs, snakes and poison ivy."

"Point…Speakin' of Holiday Inn, we can get a couple of rooms an' come back out tomorrow if they're bitin'."

"And if they're not?"

"We can still get a couple of rooms and come back out."

"Damn you, Bone, you're so full of it."

"I know. That's what makes me so lovable."

"In your dreams…What did we bring our side arms for?"

"Well, one, it's like that credit card…never go anywhere without it…and plenty of ammo. Like we say in the Marine Corps, 'no such thing as enough ammo'…but, you know those snakes you mentioned?"

"Yeah," she answered with a slight hesitation.

"This is kinda known as rattlesnake country."

"Now you tell me."

"Just watch where you step, is all. They're more afraid of you than you are of them."

"Of course they are…Just hope they know that." She set the tackle box down about ten feet from the edge of the cliff and looked out across the wide expanse of the clear blue water. "What's that?"

"What?" Bone looked up.

"That." She pointed out across the lake.

"Huh…Cloud bank. Looks like we got a fog rollin' in…or rain. Happens this time of year, you know."

"Joy…Is there anywhere around here to take cover?…Not looking forward to getting rained on. Didn't bring a change of clothes."

The big man looked around. "Looks like there's a cave in that ridge over yonder." He pointed off to their south at a dark area in a limestone outcrop.

"Think we should head on up that way?"

He looked back out over the lake at the cloud bank. "Sucker's movin' our way pretty fast…early spring storms."

They got hit with a downdraft of cold air.

"Brrr, that's a bit nippy," said Loraine as she wrapped her arms around herself. "Glad I wore a jacket."

"Yep…Means there's definitely rain in that bank."

"How do you know these things?"

He grinned at her. "It's a gift...Pick the tackle box back up. We'd best head thataway."

They grabbed the gear again and trudged toward the ridge.

"You had to bring that Thing without a top," she complained.

"Waaa, waaa, waaa, always complainin'. I'm in the process of restorin' it an' just haven't gotten around to putting the convertible top back on...Fact is, I haven't ordered it yet."

"Damn you, Bone." Loraine huffed as they started up the incline to the cave just as rain drops started to fall.

He stopped them outside the entrance.

"Why are we stopping? It's starting to rain."

Bone picked up several fist-sized rocks and pitched them inside the dark cave.

"What are you doing that for?"

"If there are any rattlers in there, that'll piss 'em off an' they'll start shakin' their tails in warnin'...We should be able to hear 'em."

"Should?"

He shrugged his wide shoulders and threw a couple more rocks.

"Well, don't hear anything. Come on."

"Maybe they're just asleep."

"That's the point of throwin' rocks."

"Right...Hey, what are those?" She pointed to several images carved into the limestone at the side of the cave.

"Huh! Indian petroglyphs...Been there a long time, I'd say."

"What do they mean?"

"Well, it's obvious that one is a buffalo." He traced the carvings with his finger. "These indicate a meteor shower...That is apparently a small person with big eyes next to a river. That one, some kind of bird...and that clockwise spiral has somethin' to do with other dimensions, worlds...or time."

"Time?"

He shook his head. "Yeah, nobody's really sure, it's just that they are found in numerous places across North and South America."

"And you know this how?"

"Like I said...it's a gift." He grinned. "Plus I watch Ancient Aliens, whenever it's on."

Loraine swatted his shoulder. "Smart ass."

Bone pulled his small military grade LED, 1000 Lumens Taclight from a pocket in his Marine Corps style BDU trousers and shined it into the back of the cave. The water-created tunnel made a turn a little over a hundred feet inside. He flashed the bright beam all along the floor.

"Well, don't see anything, I think we're in good shape here till the storm passes."

"About time…since I'm already wet."

They moved inside just as a big bolt of lightning struck the top of the ridge above their heads. They both flinched.

"Damn, I hate lightning. That one was close enough to make my skin tingle."

"Mine too."

"Hey, there's some wood against the side of the cave over there. Somebody else must have taken shelter one time or another an' left some wood…I'll build a fire."

"Anytime today, Bone. I'm freezing."

He glanced over his shoulder. "Why was it now that I brought you along?"

"You said you had a treat for me after we busted that car theft ring."

"Oh, right…Forgot," he mumbled as he stripped some bark from one of the chunks of wood for kindling.

"Uh, huh."

Bone rubbed the bark between his massive hands until it was almost a powder. He put a slab of the bark on the ground against the side of the cave and piled the light brown powder in the center. On top of that, he broke some twigs, stacked them and pulled a bic lighter from one of his big cargo pockets .

"What are you doing with a lighter? You don't smoke."

He grinned at her again. "Always carry a lighter. Never know when it'll come in handy…like now."

The dark-haired beauty frowned at him as he lit the kindling. "Did you plan all of this?"

"I'm good, Pard, but not this good."

He leaned over and blew on the tiny flame under the twigs, causing it to flare up. Bone grabbed some larger pieces of mostly driftwood and stacked them in a teepee style over the burning twigs where the dry wood quickly began to burn.

"There you go, Double D, got you a fire. You can take off your clothes and lay 'em on those rocks at the side…They'll dry in no time."

"Dream on, Bone…and don't call me Double D," she said as she moved closer to the flames and held out her hands.

"If the shoe fits, throw it at the wall," he mumbled.

"What?"

Bone looked out the entrance. "Rain's down to a heavy drizzle, but can't see three feet into the fog…Damn, that's thick. Reminds me of San Francisco."

"You've been to San Francisco?"

"No, but it reminds me of it anyway."

Loraine shook her head and grumbled, "Why me, Lord."

Several hours later the light rain had stopped and the fog was beginning to lift.

"Hey, look, I see sunshine," said Bone as he got to his feet.

Loraine followed him in rising. "Good thing, we're almost out of firewood."

Bone moved to the entrance and looked out.

"Well, damn, that's odd."

"What is?"

"The lake's gone…an' so's my Thing."

"Excuse me?"

BROKEN DIAMOND F RANCH

"Guess we oughta saddle up an' go pay our neighbors, the Sinclairs, a little friendly visit...What do you think, Marshal?"

Fiona looked out the kitchen window that faced south. "Why don't we wait till the storm passes."

"There's a storm comin'?"

"I think I said that."

"Oh, right...Maybe we have time for you to explain that Shakespeare quote to me."

She looked out the window again, and then back at Flynn, grinned and winked. "Maybe we do...Follow me, husband." She headed down the hall to their bedroom.

"Oh!...Right behind you, Pretty." He jumped to his feet and headed toward the hallway.

The dog-run style ranch house disappeared as the rain started and the dense fog rolled in.

§§§

CHAPTER FOUR

FLYING L RANCH

Slim pulled the tack on his gelding, Star, while Lisanne filled his bucket with a gallon of oats.

"Think it was Injun?" he asked.

"Couldn't tell. It was a male an' barefoot is all I know. Think if it was an Injun, he'd a been wearin' moccasins…Was considerate of him to latch the door back, though. Tracks headed toward the creek."

"'Spect he done that so's we couldn't tell 'nybody wuz in there less'n we wuz gittin' some ham, bacon er jerky our ownselves."

The Chickasaw Freedman led Star into his stall, latched the door and threw a block of hay over the top. "What say we see as we kin track 'im. My guess he didn't go too far."

"That's what I'm thinkin', too."

The sound of thunder rolled across the sky from outside. Lisanne and Slim walked to the end of the alleyway and looked off to the southwest.

"Uh, oh. That's a purty fair storm a comin'...Looky, the cloud goes all the way to the ground," said Slim.

"Yeah, so much for trackin' our thief. We better get to the house while the gettin's good...I'll go ahead and start the biscuits to go with the beans an' ham steaks...unless you'd prefer cornbread."

"Sounds good, Missy, yore biscuits is fine, 'specially with the sorghum. We kin give the creek bottom a goin' over in the later...if'n he don't git washed away."

Thunder rolled again like distant artillery as the pattering rain drops started to make little circles in the dust. The pair sprinted toward the clapboard house and cleared the four steps to the porch in one jump.

BRAZOS VALLEY

Bone pulled out the duplicate Galaxy S5 Lucy had given him to communicate with her, in 2014, activated the screen and held it up. "Yep, figured, no service...Huh, that icon of her space suit is gone...interestin'."

"Those carvings in the rock are still there," said Loraine.

He nodded. "'Spect so. Been there well over a thousand years."

They walked back over to the edge of the cliff and looked down at the Brazos River flowing below.

Bone scratched the stubble on his chin, and then turned to Loraine. "Ever read Mark Twain's *A Connecticut Yankee in King Author's Court*?"

"Can't say I have."

"Twain wrote about this engineer who receives a blow to the head knockin' him out and wakes up in the sixth century in the time of King Author an' the folks there think he's some kind of wizard."

"So?"

"Well, I think we've been transported in time back before they built the lake...Could be a hundred years...maybe more."

"Transported in time?...Time travel? Are you crazy, Bone?"

"You really want me to answer that?"

"No...but, we didn't get hit on the head, and we're both here, smart guy."

"Yeah...Don't suppose you've read Edgar Rice Burroughs' *A Princes of Mars* either?"

"Did read that one in high school. Isn't that where John Carter falls asleep or something in a cave in Arizona and wakes up naked on Mars."

"That's the one...Figured you'd remember that part."

"Damn you, Bone...You don't think we went to Mars?" she said skeptically as she swatted him across his broad chest. "Besides, those books were fiction."

"Well, most fiction is based on some kind of facts...and the western author, Ken Farmer, said 'You can often reveal the deepest truths with the lies of fiction'…Plus, I recognize those hills over yonder on the other side of the river…same as when we drove up. Just the lake an' my car is gone…We're still in Palo Pinto County, Texas, Pard ."

"But, how?"

"Your guess is good as mine…Remember that tingle we got when that lightning hit the top of the cliff…?"

"Could be…Okay, now what do we do?"

"Well, I'd say we walk back to my ranch, it's only fifty miles or so…as the crow flies."

"Joy…Glad I wore my hiking boots."

He grinned that affable grin of his. "Just a good stretch of the legs."

"Easy for you to say and wasn't that Maureen O'Hara's line from *The Quiet Man*?"

"Close enough, Pard…Probably watched it ten or twelve times. Know about every line."

She smiled. "Yeah, me too…What if the house is not there?"

"Lucy said the folks that adopted her as an abandoned orphan child a couple weeks after her ship crashed at Aurora in April of 1897…believe she said it was Cletus and Mary Lou

Wilson…bought the place in late '97. So, if it's after then, it's there…an' Lucy* is too."

Legend of Aurora - published 5/30/2014

"But, time travel?"

"She told Padrino an' me that time travel was possible, but, her people, the *Anunnaki*, could only do it on a small scale."

"How so?"

"Like when they went through a worm hole and didn't age…even though they traveled almost a hundred light years from their planet, Tyrin, to here…Somethin' 'bout Einstein's theory of relativity an' goin' faster than the speed of light. Whatever the hell that means…Said she was actually over two thousand years old."

"You're kidding."

"If I'm lyin' I'm dyin', Pard…said their life span was around four hundred years, too, but because she and her mate, Garin, made so many trips here…they were only a little over two hundred real time years old."

"Holds her age well."

"Uh, huh…What Padrino said…but, bein' only 4' 10", she was able to masquerade as an earth child without her gray space suit with the big black lenses."

"Did the Wilsons know?"

"She didn't say, but I'm bettin' they did."

"Fifty miles, huh?"

"Give or take."

"Hope it's more take than give...Oh, look down there." She pointed to an open area along the north side of the river at a herd of horses drinking.

"Wild horses used to roam this part of Texas back in the eighteenth an' nineteenth century...an' would you look at that stallion standin' guard on top of that rise behind his mares ."

"He's gorgeous. What do you call that color?"

"Steeldust."

BROKEN DIAMOND F RANCH

An exhausted Flynn rolled over from Fiona's embrace and looked out the window.

"Looks like the storm has blown over. Reckon we'd better get dressed an' make that visit."

She snuggled under his muscular arm. "You sure you don't want to go for more explanation?"

"We can save it till later…don't want you to get spoiled."

Fiona pushed his shoulder, and then rolled over to the other side of the bed. "I'll remember that…Your prevarication is going to get you into trouble, Mason Flynn."

"Do what?"

"Speaking in an evasive way."

"Oh…Well, on second thought, maybe we do have a little time."

"Little? Is that a pun?" She giggled.

"I'll show you pun, Fiona Flynn." He flipped her on top of his bare chest and covered her ruby red lips with a passionate kiss."

BAR S RANCH

Two hours later, they were traveling at a road trot toward the native stone ranch house three hundred yards in the distance. They had been on the Bar S for the last thirty minutes.

Three cowboys were loping their horses from the house toward the law officers.

Fiona and Flynn drew rein and sat their mounts in the middle of the ranch road and waited on Sinclair's hired help.

"Howdy Marshal...Sheriff, what can we do for you?" asked number two son, Rowdy, as they reined up in front of them.

Fats McClure and Jim French flanked Sinclair and moved their horses further to the sides. Fats spat a long stream of brown, viscous tobacco juice at the road.

"Just comin' to see your daddy, Slick," answered Flynn, and then glanced at the two gunhawks. "I wouldn't go any further, boys. We tend to get a might edgy when fellers with irons try to spread out."

The two men stopped, looked at each other and moved their mounts back toward number two son.

"Name's Rowdy, not Slick an' he ain't seein' guests...specially not law dogs."

"We weren't asking...*Slick*. Now I suggest you absquatulate," commented Fiona.

"What'd you call us?" questioned Rowdy.

"Didn't call you anything...yet. Just said you three miscreants need to get out of our way and do it now…Not accustomed to repeating myself," said Fiona with a sanctimonious smile.

"You be that lady marshal we've heard 'bout." Fats directed another glob of spittle toward Spot's hoof.

"I am and I don't backwater to any man." Fiona's right side Colt appeared in her hand almost as if by magic, startling the three men. "I suggest you turn and ride in front of us to your daddy's house…Now," she hissed.

"Better do what she says, girls. She can get a mite testy an' you don't want that…trust me."

FLYING L RANCH

Lisanne, carrying her double barreled .12 gauge Greener, and Slim, wearing his .44-40 Remington sidearm, worked their way through the brush and whoa vines down to the banks of Salt Creek.

"'Spect as since he's barefoot, he's a gonna stick to the game trails," said Slim as he knelt down to examine the packed earth. "Ain't nothin' been 'long here since the rain, though."

"There's a bend up the way…" She pointed left to the north. "…that might make a campsite, long as the water doesn't get too high."

"Mayhaps makes sense."

They eased along the trail and were blocked by several green thorny whoa vines.

"Well, now, this is new," whispered Lisanne.

"Uh, huh. Looks like our thief drug 'em 'cross the trail to discourage 'nybody from a comin' this a way," added Slim also sotto voce.

"Shhhh." Lisanne put her finger to her mouth and pointed up the trail on the other side of the vines.

At the bend of the creek, they could just make out a figure of a man through the budding early spring foliage sitting on a rock ledge at the edge of the creek with his feet in the water.

Slim pushed the vines down with his boot like stepping on a barb wire fence and nodded at Lisanne to step over. He eased his foot up and followed her to the small glade bordering the creek.

"How are you likin' my ham?" she asked the man from behind just as he took another bite.

The nineteen year old barefoot young man with dirty looking scraggly red hair and ragged clothes dropped the chunk of ham and jumped to his feet brandishing a kitchen knife.

"Ain't real smart bringin' a knife to a gun fight, mister," said Lisanne as she cocked both hammers of her scattergun.

§§§

CHAPTER FIVE

JACK COUNTY, TEXAS

"Suggest we avoid Jacksboro, Pard...assumin' it's there," commented Bone as they strode along to the northeast on a little used ranch road.

He carried their rods and lunch box and she had the tackle box again.

"Why?" Loraine replied.

"Well, if we did go back in time, like I think, just look at the way we're dressed...and our sidearms. Draw attention to us like turds in a punch bowl."

"Besides the obvious, that's bad because…"

"Say, it's 1898 an' people find out we're from the future?…Might be like the Salem witch trials…in addition to scarin' everybody half to death…Don't think so."

"Oh…See what you mean. Like if the public in 2014 found out that Lucy was actually an alien…Might have created a panic."

"Now you got it, Pard…We'll see if we can find some clothes of the day."

"Should be easy to find something for me, but *you'll* have to locate Omar, the tent maker."

"Maybe we can find you a saloon girl's outfit," he quipped as he walked away.

"Damn you, Bone." She swatted him across the back.

Several hours later they came to a well-traveled dirt road with multiple wagon wheel tracks.

Bone looked both ways. "Five'll get you ten this road runs between Fort Worth an' Jacksboro, probably became Highway 199 in our time…Reasonable amount of traffic, looks like. We'll cross it an' keep headin' to the northea…"

He was interrupted by the sound of a shotgun from just around a bend in the road to the southeast. A dense copse of post oak shielded their view.

"Bird hunter?" asked Loraine.

"Not likely, not this time of year…We'd best check it out. Sounded like a twelve gauge." He started out in the direction of the shot, followed by Loraine.

"We going through the woods?"

"Best way…Safest, too," he replied.

They worked their way through the six inch diameter oaks until they could see a stagecoach being pulled by six horses stopped in the middle of the road.

There were four men wearing bandanas over the lower half of their faces. One, standing in front and to the side of the team, had a shotgun, its stock resting on his hip, the twin barrels pointed in the air. The other three, held revolvers, pointing at the driver and messenger seated atop the stage.

The man with the shotgun shouted at the two men, "Awright, messenger, throw down that coach gun of yore's. Jehu, you chunk down yer

Winchester, the box an' the mail pouch…an' do it now. You folks inside git out an' don't 'nybody do 'nythin' stupid an' nobody gits hurt." He fired the other barrel of his Remington twelve gauge in the air.

The express messenger pitched his sawed-off double-barreled ten gauge to the ground and raised his hands.

The leader broke his scattergun open and reloaded it as the passengers stepped out. The driver threw his rifle, strong box and mail pouch down.

Three men, one a rancher, another a business man and the third, a garishly dressed drummer, got out. The rancher turned and offered his hand to a young dark-haired woman as she stepped down the two metal steps to the ground.

Two of the men with the handguns moved toward the passengers while the other went to the box and mail pouch.

"Huh, looks just like a scene from a Brad Dennison or Ken Farmer western novel…Guess it gives us a general idea as to when we are. That was a 1886 Winchester the driver dropped to the dirt," whispered Bone as he nodded at Loraine for them to spread out.

One of the outlaws, a small, skinny man, confronting the passengers, strode to the woman and jerked a cameo broach hanging from her neck, breaking the thin gold chain.

"Haw! Looky what I got. My gal…"

He was interrupted by an extremely loud explosion, an instantaneous metallic *blang*, followed by a piercing scream from the leader.

The three outlaws, the passengers, and then the driver and messenger looked first at the boss, and then at the giant of a man at the edge of the trees holding a very large stainless-steel revolver.

"All right, that's enough," boomed the big man.

The leader was screaming and holding his numbed, bleeding hand which now was missing his trigger finger that had been inside the demolished trigger guard. Then they looked at the man holding the huge handgun with a tiny tendril of smoke curling from the massive barrel.

The outlaw's double-barreled shotgun lay on the ground, blown into two pieces, separated at the receiver.

"Ow, ow, ow, my hand, my hand," he screamed as he danced around, and then looked at the big man. "What the hell is that cannon you shot me with?"

"Oh, just the most powerful handgun in the world, a .50 caliber Smith and Wesson with a seven inch barrel…Does a good job, don't it?" said Bone with a big grin.

".50 caliber? Jesus, H!…The hell you say…No matter, we got you outnumbered and outgunned, anyway, man-mountain," said the skinny one still holding the cameo as he and the others pointed their pistols at Bone.

"Oh, I wouldn't say that," came a feminine voice from the back of the stage.

Everyone, but Bone, spun around to see Loraine with her Kimber pointed in their direction.

"This is a .45 caliber, semiautomatic handgun, with an eight round capacity, children. It'll fire as fast as I can squeeze the trigger. That means you'll all be dead before you can get off a shot…but better me than his .50 cal…don't you think?"

"Damnation, I heard tell of them automatic shooters," muttered one of the outlaws to the others.

"Now drop your weapons…all of 'em." Bone cocked the massive five shot revolver.

The three pistols hitting the hard-packed road made but a single sound.

"The hideouts and knives, too," said Loraine.

The wounded leader lifted his sidearm from its holster with two fingers of his left hand, dropped it to the ground, and then pulled his Bowie and let it fall beside it. The others followed suit with two derringers, a snub-nosed Webley Bulldog and three knives hitting the dirt.

"Driver, if ya'll have some rope or extra leather straps, I'd suggest you bind these hooligans up so they stay out of mischief. Then load 'em on top...I'm sure the sheriff in the next town will be glad to take 'em off your hands."

Bone looked at the rancher. "Friend, why don't you gather up the weaponry and put it inside the stage. Don't think they'll be needin' 'em for quite a spell."

"Is somebody gonna wrap my hand before I bleed to death?" whined the leader, holding his bleeding hand.

Loraine stepped over and jerked the wildrag from around his neck and looked over at the drummer. "You mind wrapping this around his stub?"

"But that thing's dirty," complained the leader.

Loraine cut her dark brown eyes at the outlaw. "You don't say?" She walked back over to Bone as he took the cameo from the skinny outlaw's hand and gave it back to the woman.

"You'll have to get that chain fixed, Ma'am," he said.

"Thank you, kind sir," the attractive woman flashed him a smile, nodded and slipped the necklace into her small black velvet clutch.

The driver looked at Bone. "Just want to thank you, mister...You too, ma'am. But, who are ya'll anyway?"

They exchanged glances.

"They call me Bone...She's my partner, Loraine...We're cops."

"Ya'll need a ride? We're headed to Jacksboro," said the driver.

"No thanks, we're headed a different direction," answered Loraine.

"We'll find their horses and use them...ya'll don't mind," said Bone.

"Shore, fair enough," said the driver.

Loraine and Bone crossed the road behind the stage and disappeared into the post oaks after they had helped load the robbers on top.

The driver and messenger exchanged glances.

"Well, don't that beat all...Reckon Sheriff Flynn'll believe us?" asked the messenger.

The driver glanced at the passengers stepping back up into the stage, and then at the four trussed-up outlaws piled on top. "He'll believe all of us, I mind."

He flicked the ribbons over the tops of the horses and cracked his whip in the air. "Hyaah...Git up there you slab-sided cayuses."

The six horses surged against the heavily weighted stage until momentum caught up with them and they trotted on toward Jacksboro in a cloud of dust.

Bone and Loraine watched the stage disappear around the bend from the trees. They picked up their lunch box and fishing gear and headed across the road.

"Thought I heard a horse nicker over yonder." He pointed to the other side of a grove of junipers.

"Damn sure'll beat walking," commented Loraine. "My feet are already killing me." She glanced at Bone. "Why didn't you just kill that leader? He was going to shoot the driver and shotgun messenger."

"Don't know, except I remember an episode of *Star Trek Voyager* where they talked about interferin' with the space-time continuum."

He pushed through the cedars to the four horses tied to limbs. "...If we do somethin' like kill somebody in this time period, it could have major changes as to what happens to the future. It's called the temporal paradox."

"Temporal paradox?"

"Yeah, like if say we cause the death of my grandfather or great grandfather...I would never be born."

"Doesn't sound like too bad an idea."

"Bite me...We're not really supposed to be here, you know."

"If that's right...then why are we?"

Bone shook his head and raised his eyebrows as he adjusted the stirrups on a sorrel mare for her. "Good question, Pard, good question...Hope Lucy's here, maybe we can find out...and how we can get back to our time."

He tied their fishing gear and lunch box to the Texas style saddle on a bay gelding, by the long saddle strings.

"What if it's not quite 1897 and Lucy's not here yet?" Loraine commented as she stepped up into the mare's saddle

"Guess we wait." Bone's bronze eyes twinkled as he swung easily onto the back of a sixteen hand blazed-face black gelding.

§§§

CHAPTER SIX

BAR S RANCH

Mason and Fiona calmly sat their horses in front of Sinclair's porch as the patriarch of the clan opened the screen door and stepped out. He held a tumbler of scotch in one hand and a lit, hand-wrapped Cuban cigar between the fingers of his other.

Rowdy and the two gunhands dismounted, tied their mounts to hitch rails, stepped up on the porch and stood to the side of Sinclair.

Frenchy took out his makings and rolled himself a cigarette.

"Sheriff...Ma'am. What can I do for you?" asked Algernon.

"First off, don't call me Ma'am. It's Marshal or even Missus Flynn..."

The sheriff took over, "...and second we want to know why your hired help took a shot at Lisanne Gifford, Slim Parker and me this mornin'."

Sinclair chuckled. "Oh, didn't know ya'll were married. Congratulations, I'm sure," he said almost politely. "You must be mistaken, Sheriff. My men wouldn't do that."

"Not in the habit of bein' mistaken about bein' shot at, Sinclair. The tracks of the two men led right here."

"Well, I did have two men out this mornin'. They were lookin' for wild horses." He looked over at Frenchy and Fats. "Those two right there, actually and I'm sure any rifle fire in your direction was an accident...That right, boys?"

"That's right, boss. We seen a coyote an Fats here took a shot at it, but missed...Critter took off like he was scalded," said Big Jim as he chuckled and took a drag from his roll-your-own.

"That's right," concurred Fats, he spat a stream of tobacco juice to the ground beside the porch.

Mason and Fiona exchanged glances, and then he looked at Frenchy.

"You got'ny' more fixin's?"

The hired hand pulled a Bull Durham sack from his pocket. "Shore, Sheriff, need to roll yerself a quirly?" He walked toward the edge of the porch to hand the sack to Mason.

"Nope…Don't smoke."

Frenchy stopped and looked puzzled. "Then why…"

Mason fished a butt he had picked up that morning from his vest pocket. "You left a couple of butts where you two were waitin' to take a shot at us." He held one up. "Bull Durham." He glanced at Fats. "Plus there were numerous chaw stains on the side of the boulder an' in the dirt where ya'll were hidin'…Not countin' this." He pulled out a brass .45-70 casing and rolled it between his fingers.

Fiona looked at Algernon. "I'd say your gunhawks there lied to you, Sinclair…or were they just doing what they were told?"

"Hey, woman, you cain't call us liars," shouted Fats as he spat another noxious stream of tobacco juice for emphasis.

"This Deputy United States Marshal's badge I'm wearing says I can call you anything I damn well please…and it doesn't matter if I stand or squat to pee."

"Now, I'd watch my mouth, Fats, she don't take no sass…not even from me," commented Flynn.

He turned to Sinclair. "We were just about to catch that steeldust stallion, when we were fired upon…I'm tempted to call that attempted murder of a peace officer…"

"And that makes it my jurisdiction," added Fiona.

Sinclair threw his half-smoked cigar to the side. "Now see here, law officer or no, we got just as much right to catch that wild stallion as anybody…and we aim to do it!" He jutted his jaw out.

"Yes, you do, but you interfere with that little girl catchin' him an' you're gonna deal not only with me, but the United States government, too." He glanced at Fiona.

"Are we clear?" asked Fiona with fire in her steel-gray eyes.

"I don't take kindly to threats," hissed Sinclair.

Fiona looked at him with a wry smile. "Not a threat...'Such antics do not amount to a man.' - Shakespeare, *Henry V*...Shall we go, Sheriff Flynn?"

"I think so, Marshal Flynn."

They reined their mounts about and nudged them into a trot toward the Bar S entrance.

Sinclair's flush of anger slowly subsided as he took a sip of his scotch.

Rowdy looked at him. "What did she mean, Pa?"

Sinclair glared at his second born, slugged the remaining scotch down, spun on his heel and went back inside. "Idiots."

Fats spat off the porch again. "Guess he don't know either, Rowdy."

FLYING L RANCH

"Now what are you doin' stealin' our food?" asked Lisanne.

The young man's eyes welled up as he looked at his bare feet. "I…I was just hungry, Miss…I'm powerful sorry…Haven't eaten in three days." He looked up with tear lines down his cheeks, bent over and picked up a dirty flour sack and held it out to Lisanne. "Here. God as my witness, didn't eat…" He swallowed. "…much. Just couple bites of the ham." He swallowed again. "It was shore good."

Lisanne turned away as her own eyes filled and she glanced over at Slim. He was tearing up, also and looked down at the ground.

"Damn," she said softly.

"Miss?" he questioned when he couldn't hear her. "Please take it back…I never stole nuthin 'fore." He held the sack out again. "I'm a good worker…I'll work it out…Can I?"

Lisanne dried her eyes with the back of her knuckles, took a deep breath and turned back around.

"Uh, what's your name?"

"Buster…Buster Martin. Least my mama an' papa always called me Buster. Guess that was it 'cause I always came when they called it."

She choked back a smile, at least most of it. "Well, Buster, tell you what do...Just so happens we've been lookin' for some more hired-help..."

"Miss Lisanne..."

"Hush, Slim..." She turned back to Buster. "You can work out your room, board and found of a dollar a week...How's that sound?"

"Oh, Miss..." Buster choked back a sob, fell to his knees, his body shaking with tears.

"Miss Lisanne?"

She turned to the black man. "What, Slim?"

"Wuz jest gonna say, could use somebody to help with muckin' the foalin' stalls an' sech...Plus the spring needs a cleanin' out."

She hugged the skinny man's neck and whispered, "Thank you."

Lisanne turned back again, took Buster's arm and helped him to his feet. "Enough of that now. Come on, you got work to do...Need to get you some shoes, too."

The young man's voice broke with emotion as he tried to respond, "Yes, miss...I'm ready." He looked at her with his dirty tear-streaked face. "I don't know what to say."

They started walking back toward the ranch.

"What happened to your mama and daddy?" she asked.

He pursed his lips as his eyes filled again. "Some men come by our place last week an' tol' Pa we was squattin' an' we had to git out...Their boss needed the grass for his horses."

Lisanne looked over at Slim.

"Pa tol' 'em we was homesteadin' that land an' sides we didn't have but six cows an' a bull." He took a breath. "He tol' 'em to go pound sand...an' they shot 'im, right then an' there...They shot 'im...Fetched 'im dead."

Tears began to roll down his face again. "I was out in the barn, tryin' to fix a ol' hand plow for mama's garden..."

"Where was your mama?" asked Lisanne.

"Inside, bakin' bread...When she heard the shot, she come runnin' out an'...an' they shot her too...Oh, God!" He dropped to his knees again and sobbed unabashedly.

"It's goin' to be all right, Buster," she said through her own tears. "Goin' to be all right."

Slim had stopped an leaned his hand against a tree and just stared at the ground.

Buster raised up and shook his head. "Then they went an' set fire to the house…an' rode off laughin'."

He stopped and looked up at her, and then over at Slim. "My sister…My baby sister was…was inside in her crib." He choked back another sob. "By the time they rode off an' I run to the house…it…it was too late…I couldn't git to her…The fire…I…I let her die…Don'tcha see? I let her die!…I let my baby sister die!"

He collapsed to the ground again.

Lisanne pulled him to his feet, wrapped her arms around him and held him tight to her. "Let it go, Buster, let it go…You did what you could…No way you could save her."

"Shoulda just run in that fire an' died too…Don't deserve to live." His body shook with his guilt.

"No, Buster, that would have been a sin. You got to go on." She leaned back, held both his shoulders and looked him in the eyes. "Honor them with your life…I lost my mama, daddy and baby brother, too. I know what you're goin' through…This will pass. Trust me."

She took his hand. "Now come on. We'll go to the house an' I'll fix some supper. Already got some red beans on."

He dried his eyes with the sleeves of his filthy shirt, nodded and walked with her and Slim up the path back to the ranch.

JACK COUNTY, TEXAS

"What are these rifles in the scabbards," asked Loraine as they walked their horses along the road.

Bone glanced over. "Well, yours is a '66 Yellowboy, shoots .44 rimfire. Bet there's some ammo in the saddlebags behind your butt."

He looked down at the stock sticking out of his boot and pulled the rifle out. "Ha! Mine's a '86 Winchester...an' Lord love a duck....45-70 Government center fire. Hotdamn...drop a buffalo at five hundred yards...if there are any."

"Sun's going down. We're not going to ride on in the dark, are we?"

"Nope. Gonna find some place with water an' grass for the horses...Good thing I brought the lunch box."

"What's in it?"

"Food fit for a king, M'lady…peanut butter and jelly sandwiches, sardines and cheese and cracker lunchables…Oh, yeah…couple bags of corn nuts an' candy corn…All we need is some beer."

Loraine shook her head. "My sweet Lord in Heaven…It's a wonder your arteries can still pump blood."

He chuckled. "They're afraid not to."

"I can believe it."

JACKSBORO, TEXAS

Mason and Fiona rode up to Mom Tucker's Livery at the end of the main street and dismounted. The fiftyish, stocky woman dressed in her usual blue bib overalls and with a smoldering corn cob pipe in her mouth, stepped out of the wide alleyway.

"Well, my favorite law officers. How's the new married couple this fine afternoon?" She took the reins to Flynn's blue roan Morgan gelding, Laddie, and Fiona's painted John mule, Spot.

"Fine, Mom," replied Fiona.

"Ya'll stayin' over the night? Little late to be headin' out to yore ranch, ain't it?"

"I'd say," said Mason. "Figured we'd supper at Ruth Ann's, spell Gomer an' earn my pay doin' rounds this evenin'."

"He's a changed boy since ya'll got back from the Territory with his intended, Emma Lou. She's such a sweety. Started workin' at Ruth Ann's today."

"Oh, good. It was easy to tell right off that they were made for each other...It didn't take them long to realize it, either." Fiona glanced over at Mason. "Not like somebody I know."

He looked at her from loosening Laddie's cinch. "Huh?"

She turned back to Mom. "See."

"Uh, huh...Not surprised...He's a man." She turned with their mounts toward the barn. "I'll take care of that, Sheriff. Ya'll can head on down to Sewel's. She's got fried chicken, buttered squash, taters an' gravy...an' yeast rolls for the supper special an' with apple cobbler for desert."

"Yum," replied Mason. "I'm starvin'."

"When aren't you?" Fiona took his elbow and they headed toward the restaurant.

They had only gotten a block when the sound of the Fort Worth stage thundering into town from the southeast caused them to stop.

"What the Sam Hill…" Flynn exclaimed as he noted the four bound men on top of the stage behind the driver and shotgun messenger, Charlie Mitchell and Pearly Clark.

"Ho, up there, boys. Ho, up there," hollered Charlie as he pulled back on the multiple reins to the six horses and eased the brake lever forward with his right foot.

The coach rolled to a stop in front of the stage depot adjacent to Sewel's, just past Jack Street, followed by clouds of billowing dust.

Charlie spotted Mason and Fiona headed down the boardwalk almost to the cafe. "Sheriff, got some miscreants fer ya."

"Tried to hold us up, they did," added Pearly.

"What do you mean, 'tried'," asked the sheriff.

Charlie stepped down to the boardwalk and turned to help Pearly lower the tied up outlaws to the street.

"I'll be damned, you got Wild Bob an' his gang. How the devil…" said Mason as he stepped up to help with the outlaws.

"What I wuz fixin' to tell you…This go-liath of a man with a real short haircut, an' a good lookin' Mezcan woman, dressed kindly funny, they was…Both was wearin' pants what was several different colors in splotches, with big pockets on the side…Wellsir, them two stepped out of the brush 'bout ten miles outta town and stopped them malefactors right in the middle of the holdup…" Charlie started.

"He blowed Wild Bob's shotgun plumb in two…Shot his fanger off in the process," added Pearly.

"What do you mean, 'blowed the shotgun in two'?" asked Fiona.

Charlie took off his hat and wiped his brow with his bandana. "Just that, Marshal. This giant had what he said was a .50 caliber Smith and Wesson revolver…Looked like a goldang cannon…sounded like one too, I'm here to say…"

Pearly interrupted him. "The woman held what she called a .45 semiautomatic with eight rounds…an' it weren't no revolver."

".50 caliber Smith and Wesson revolver? No such thing."

"Thought so, too, Sheriff, but that's what it was, no doubt about it. Didn't shoot no buckshot like a LaMat, neither…Big as it was, looked like a toy in that big son of a gun's hand," said Charlie.

"That man-mountain said his name was Bone an' hers was Loraine…an' that they was cops!" added Pearly.

"Cops?" asked Fiona.

§§§

CHAPTER SEVEN

FLYING L RANCH

"Here's a old pair of brogans...belonged to my ex-step daddy an' his extra set of overalls an' union suit...He won't be needin' 'em where he went."

"Thankee kindly...Where'd he go?" asked Buster.

"I' 'spect where all bad men go. The army hung him last month for desertin'. He wasn't no count anyways...Those shoes fit?"

He slipped the worn ankle-length coarse stout Thomas Jefferson brogan on his right foot and nodded. "Just a little loose, but they'll do fine."

She dug into a drawer of an old chifferobe and pulled out a pair of worn once white cotton socks. "Here, these should help."

"Gollydang, ain't never had 'ny socks before…thanks again."

"Now go out to the water trough by the barn, wash up, get out of those raggedy clothes an' put these things on. I've got to get the ham steaks an' biscuits on…Think I'll make some buttermilk cornbread, too…An' don't get any soap in the trough." She handed him a bar of homemade lye soap, a clean wash rag and a towel. "Use the dipper to rinse with."

He nodded and his eyes welled up again as he grabbed the clothes from the bed. "I don't know how to thank you, Miss. I…"

"Now, don't start that again. Was gonna throw that stuff out anyways. Here's a comb, too…scat." She shooed him toward the door.

In twenty minutes Buster came back in the house, his freckled face fairly shining from the recent scrubbing.

"Well, you look like a different feller," said Slim.

His red hair was still a little wet, but parted in the middle and combed down smooth.

"My, my, those clothes even fit fairly well...and don't you look nice," added Lisanne.

He blushed and scuffed the floor with his shoes. "Feels kinda good to be clean again."

"'Cleanliness is next to Godliness', says in the good book," said Lisanne as she took the pan of hot biscuits from the oven and set them in a plate on the table next to the butter and a quart mason jar of sorghum.

"Sorghum! You got sorghum...Oh, wow. Biscuits, butter an' sorghum's good a desert as there is."

"Go along with that, youngster," said Slim as he pulled out a chair from under the table and nodded toward another one. "Have a sit."

Lisanne grinned as she set three plates on the table with still sizzling ham steaks followed by a fragrant steaming bowl of red beans.

She sat down at one of the two remaining slat-back chairs. "All right, boys, dig in...Don't expect to see anythin' left, either."

Barney laid down next to her chair.

"Don't have to say that twice, Miss," said Buster with a big grin.

Lisanne emptied a couple ladles of beans on her plate, grabbed a wedge of cornbread and crumbled it over them. "Know anything about horses, Buster?" she asked as she mixed the cornbread in.

He looked up with a mouthful of ham and swallowed. "Uh...not much, Miss. We didn't even have a plow horse."

"That's awright, sonny, druther learn you right to start with, 'stead of tryin' to fix what you been doin' wrong," said Slim.

"I can milk, though."

"That's a good job for you to start with. Cassie likes a easy hand," commented Lisanne.

JACK COUNTY, TEXAS

"Well, that would be Boons Creek, is my guess. Me and Captain St. John fished it a time or two...Good place to set up camp," said Bone as he looked out over the forty-foot wide creek from the small glade, reined up on the black gelding and dismounted.

"Creek's a whole lot cleaner than in our time...actually see the limestone bottom." He unloaded the fishing gear. "Maybe we can go fishin' in the mornin'. Nice mess of bass or blue cat would taste good for breakfast."

"Oooh, that does sound good...How much further you think to the ranch?"

"About twenty miles, I'd say. Should make it sometime tomorrow, now that we got horses...Hey, there's a fire pit somebody before us left...Bless their hearts."

"Guess that means sleeping on the ground?...With the fire ants?" asked Loraine.

"Not any fire ants. There weren't in this country till they were accidentally brought here from South America in the 1930s...And don't worry about sleepin' on the ground, Pard."

He pointed over at some large pecan trees nearby. "You could always climb one of those big pecan trees over there and straddle a limb...I'd be careful about noddin' off to sleep, though...

"One of these days I'm going to kill you, Bone."

He chuckled. "I'll show you how to comfy the ground up with some cedar branches. Makes a real nice bed."

"Yeah, right."

"I'm guessin' these rolls behind our saddles have ground tarps an' blankets."

"Did you smell those guys? They weren't too friendly with soap and water."

"And don't forget the lice."

Loraine hung her head. "Oh, God," she said as she stepped down from her saddle.

"I'll get a fire started after I water an' hobble the horses on some grass. Figure it's goin' to get a bit nippy tonight...'specially if you decide not to cover up with one of those blankets...Oh, go through those saddlebags, while you're restin', see about any ammo and bet one of 'em has some coffee and a pot...Might be some food, too."

"Anything would beat sardines and cheese and crackers."

"Beggars can't be choosers." He started pulling the tack from the animals and stacking it near the fire pit.

STEELDUST

SEWEL'S CAFE

"Charlie, you an' Pearly come by the office after you eat and write up a report for me...Hate to hold ya'll up, but you got it to do, boys...an' bring all those guns to the office, too...Be interested in knowin' a little more about those two cops...an' their weapons."

"Understand, Sheriff. Needin' to rest my backside a little anyhoo...Sure the Breckenridge bound passengers won't mind the extra rest from that rough coach, neither," said Charlie.

Sheriff Flynn nodded at them as he and Fiona headed over to their regular table against the far wall. They had just seated themselves when the waitress walked up.

Sheriff Flynn...Fiona, or should I say, Miz Flynn, good to see ya'll."

"Thank you Emma Lou, wonderful to see you, too. Your hair looks so nice," said Fiona. "And you can call me most anything, but Ma'am."

"Thank you, uh, Marshal." She blushed and pulled at one of the red spring curls on the side of her head and held up her note pad. "What can I get ya'll?"

"Still got 'ny of the special left?" asked Mason.

"Oh, yessir, you know Ruth Ann, she always fixes plenty."

"That good for you, Honey?" asked Mason.

"Sounds wonderful. Love her chicken."

"Tea for both of you?"

The sheriff nodded. "Sweet an' a sprig of mint."

"Comin' right up." The freckled-faced, waspwaisted, teenager grinned, spun on her heel and headed toward the kitchen.

"Oh, an' see if Ruth Ann's got any scraps or steak bones for Newton."

"You got it." She brushed her fingertips on her betrothed, Gomer Platt's shoulder as he was finishing his apple cobbler desert. He looked up and winked at her. Emma Lou blushed again and continued to the kitchen.

"Make a good pair," said the sheriff.

"They do, don't they?" added Fiona.

"What do you think about those two cops?"

"Well, the fact that they called themselves, 'cops', tells me they're from a city or at least a town large enough where they have a police department."

"What the hell does 'cop' stand for, anyway? I've heard it was Constable on Patrol or that many sheriff's badges were made of copper."

"The entomology dates back to the sixteenth century from a Dutch word *capere*…meaning 'to capture or grab'. It has now become synomous with 'police officer' or even 'law officer'," said Fiona.

Mason shook his head. "So we're 'cops', too?"

"You could say so."

"You amaze me at what you know."

They looked up as Emma set their iced tea on the table. "Bring your plates in a jiffy."

"Thank you," said Mason.

She looked back over at her handsome husband and grinned. "I read a lot."

"Right" He paused and took a drink from his tea glass. "My gut tells me we haven't seen the last of those 'cops'."

BAR S RANCH

"Carter take a couple of the boys and see about trackin' down that wild horse herd in the mornin'."

"What about that stallion, Pa?"

The patriarch dropped his head and stared at his supper plate for a moment, and then looked up. "Carter, doesn't it stand to reason that if you find that herd of mares, the stallion won't be too far away?"

"Oh, right...Makes sense." Carter wiped his plate with a biscuit and stuffed it in his mouth.

"Glad somethin' does," his father muttered.

"What's that, Pa?" He looked up after swallowing.

"Nothin'....Just try to drive 'em to that box canyon near the east side of the ranch. Get 'em in there an' block off the entrance...You should be able to throw a loop on that rank son of a bitch an' tie him to one of those railroad ties we scattered around."

"'Bout a week of draggin' one of those hundered pound ties around'll take the rank out of 'im, I'll wager," said Rowdy.

"I imagine there's a few of those mares we can use, too."

Al nodded. "Some of 'em look purty shiny, Pa...I'd say you were right."

"You think?" said the old man, sarcastically.

He turned back to Carter. "What about those squatters over that direction?"

The youngest Sinclair wiped his mouth on his sleeve. "Uh…They ain't there no more, Pa…We burnt the house down after they, uh, left."

"Do you ever think about your actions before you do them?"

"Huh? Uh, shore, Pa. Why, just the other day…"

"We could've used that house for a line shack…Think about that?"

Carter stared at the coffee cup in his hand. "Oh…yeah. Right, Pa…We didn't burn the barn, though." He looked up and grinned.

The head of the clan threw his napkin in his plate and got to his feet. "Wonders never cease," he muttered through gritted teeth, as he left the room.

§§§

CHAPTER EIGHT

FLYING L RANCH

"Coffee hits the spot after that scrumptious supper, Miss Lisanne," said Buster as he sipped his coffee and rocked in one of the slat-backed rocking chairs on the front porch.

"Hard to tell if'n you liked her cookin', though," commented Slim as he packed his old briar pipe.

"May not even have to wash his plate," added Lisanne.

"Huh?…My momma always wash…" He blushed. "Ya'll are funnin' with me, ain'tcha?"

"Boy's sharper'n a tack, ain't he, Lisanne?"

She giggled. "He doesn't miss much…At least we'll have hot buttermilk biscuits for breakfast…There wasn't even a single crumb left in the pan."

"Dang! An' I'm kindly partial to cold biscuits and butter, too," exclaimed Slim as he lit his pipe and blew a light blue cloud of the aromatic maple flavored smoke over his head.

"See I'm gonna have to be on my toes around you two." Buster grinned.

"Figured we better break you in right, if you're goin' to be stayin' around here." Lisanne smiled back. "We try to not take anythin' serious but the horses."

"I can understand that," he replied.

"There's an empty bunk in the new bunkhouse we just built. Eventually see havin' three to four more hands as we build up the herd…Breakfast is at sunup," said Lisanne.

"Yes, Miss…Believe I'll sit a while longer here on the porch with this larripin' good coffee." He held up the blue speckled graniteware cup.

"You do what you please. I'm hittin' the sack…Gonna go trackin' a wild stallion an' his herd of mares we're wanting to add after breakfast while you an' Slim work on the fencin' for the mare pasture."

Barney got to his feet and followed Lisanne into the house.

JACK COUNTY

After the sun went down, Bone and Loraine sat by a roaring fire of driftwood, sipping coffee and looking up at the sky.

"Never seen stars like that," said Loraine as she gazed up at the millions upon millions specks of light that looked like tiny flickering campfires in the moonless black velvet sky.

"Got too much light pollution back in our time…this is a whole 'nuther world…or guess I should say, time."

"Well, you were right about one thing," said Loraine.

"And that would be?"

"There was coffee, a pot and some cups. Don't think I've ever had any quite this strong, though."

"Put hair on your chest, Pard."

"Pass."

"Padrino taught me how to make trail coffee…Think one of the first brands was called Arbuckle…Have to bring it to a boil twice before the grounds will sink to the bottom an' it's ready."

"Can't believe we cooked in that nasty-assed skillet," she said as she took another sip.

"Fire was hot enough to kill most anything, I imagine. The bacon and canned beans were good, though…and the pickled peaches hit the spot, too. Like I said earlier, all we were missin' was some beer."

He paused, blew across the top of his cup and took a sip of his coffee. "For some reason, most anything tastes better cooked over a campfire out in the boonies…'Specially that home-cured bacon. Beats the hell out of that stuff the supermarkets sell in our time…all pumped full of water, salt an' other chemicals."

"Why do they inject water in bacon anyway?" asked Loraine.

"That's easy…To carry the chemicals, plus it's sold by the pound and the water increases the weight…It cures it overnight."

"How was that bacon we just ate cured?"

"In these days, they hung bacon, hams, sausage, jerky and other meats in a small wooden building with a slow burnin' fire of hickory or mesquite for three to four weeks…A smoke house, if you will."

"Sure makes a difference in how it tastes."

"You think?"

A coyote in the distance started yapping. Numerous others joined in their song creating a cacophony of yips and howls.

"What is that?" Loraine said, sitting up and looking out into the inky darkness.

"Boy, I can tell you've never been campin' before…That's coyotes. They're packin' up an' singin' campfire songs before they go on the hunt."

"Uh, huh."

"They usually wait till the moon comes up, but since there's not one tonight, they can see our fire an' it makes 'em want to tune up."

"Bone, you are so full of it…What are they going to hunt?"

"Oh, mostly rabbits, coons, squirrels, nestin' birds...good lookin', big-breasted Mexican women...You know?"

She picked up a rock and threw it at him.

He ducked. "Missed."

"Damn you, Bone...Just wait till you go to sleep, big guy. Pay backs are hell."

"Uh, oh."

JACKSBORO, TEXAS

"Gomer, you can go ahead and take off," Mason said as he poured cups of coffee at the potbellied stove in the corner for Fiona and himself.

"'Preciate it, Sheriff." He got up from behind his desk in the sheriff's office and laid down a copy of the Police Gazette he had been reading.

"The marshal an' I will do the rounds. I imagine Emma will be wantin' you to escort her to the boardin' house when she gets off work."

He blushed. "Yessir, she ain't much for walkin' alone in the dark."

"You're just the man to remedy that aren't you?" said Fiona.

His blush deepened as he nodded, grinned and headed toward the door.

Newton woofed at him.

"Your hat, Gomer. Don't forget your hat," commented Mason.

He stopped and wheeled toward the hat tree in the corner of the office. "Yessir." Platt grabbed his worn gray Stetson, shoved it on his head and turned again toward the door.

"Your gunbelt, Deputy," added Fiona. "Law officer's not much count without his sidearm this day and time, is he?"

He hung his head and stepped over to the row of wooden pegs next to the gunrack, grabbed his belt gun, buckled it around his trim waist and looked around the office to see if he had forgotten anything else.

"That should have it. Ya'll have a nice evenin', hear?"

"Yessir, Sheriff." He tipped his hat to Fiona. "Marshal...Ya'll too."

When the door was finally closed behind the deputy, Mason turned to Fiona. "Gonna have to tie kerosene rags around his ankles to keep the sugar ants off'n him…Boy's as lovestruck as I've ever seen."

"I think it's sweet."

"That's my point." He reached for her tiny waist. "Come here, Missus Flynn." Mason pulled her close to him and kissed her tenderly.

"Thought we'd never be alone, Mister Flynn," she said as she kissed him back.

Newton laid down on the floor next to the stove and placed both paws over his nose—he jerked his head up and looked toward the door at the report of a gunshot from outside.

"Ah, damn…That's from the Coolwater Saloon."

Mason grabbed a double-barreled coach gun from the gunrack and nodded at the door. "After you, Marshal."

She held the door open. "Stay here, Newton."

"Let him come. A growlin' dog can be just as effective on settlin' a disturbance as a shotgun, sometimes."

"As you wish, Sheriff."

Flynn followed her and Newton out the door and down the street toward the Coolwater, which was across the street from the cafe.

They approached the batwing doors of the saloon, Flynn motioned Fiona to the other side and looked over the top. He held up two fingers and pushed his way inside. She followed and took a position behind and to his left.

Newton padded alongside as Flynn stopped and thumbed back both hammers...

Two cowboys standing in front of the bar, each with guns in their hands, heard the ominous sounds from the doorway accompanied by a low throaty growl and turned simultaneously.

"Don't think you boys want me to use this...do ya?"

"Uh, Sheriff Flynn," said the nearest one, wobbling slightly. He cut his eyes to Fiona on the floor side opposite from the bar. "Uh...Marshal Flynn."

She nodded at the inebriated cowboy with a wry grin.

The second cowboy spoke up, "He spilt my drank, Sheriff."

"And this nabob smartmouthed me," said the first.

"Who fired the shot?"

"I did, Sheriff," said the first cowboy looking down at the sawdust floor.

"An' missed, you jackanape…cain't hit a bull in the butt with a broom."

"Just who are you two. I can't seem to call your names," said Flynn.

The second cowboy said, "I'm Stoner Abbot…an' he's my baby brother Archie." He grinned. "It's really Archabald, but he don't like it much, prefers Archie…We work out at the Circle R."

"You shut yer damn pie hole…I'll stomp a mudhole in yer ass deep enough to bury a wagon."

"Not in this lifetime, you…"

"Awright, awright. That's enough…Lay those irons on the bar, an' then shake hands," said the Sheriff.

They did as they were told, turned, faced each other and stuck out their hands. Instead of shaking, they hugged each other.

"I'm sorry, brother," said Archie.

"Me too…Glad you missed," said Stoner as the brothers pounded each other's back.

"I'm drunk as a skunk," added Archie, with a grin. "An' yer right, I'd a plumb missed a barn."

"I know," said Stoner. He turned to the sheriff. "Reckon we oughta go down to yer jail an' sleep it off?"

"I'd say…Gonna have to charge you with disturbin' the peace…mine." He turned aside. "Now, march. The jail is one block west. Go to the back, pick an empty cell, go in…an' stay there…Got that?"

"Yessir," they said in unison as they staggered arm-in-arm to the door.

"You gonna come down an' lock us in?" asked Stoner.

"No…I said stay there…didn't I?"

"Oh, right…Come on baby brother."

They tipped their hats at Fiona on the way. She nodded back at them.

The middle-aged, balding owner, Truman, bent over and placed his forehead on his polished bar top and laughed until tears ran down his cheeks. The rest of the patrons of the Coolwater Saloon joined in.

Truman raised up and wiped his cheeks. "That was about the funniest thing I ever seen, Sheriff, bar none…'an' stay there', haw…Drinks on the house."

Mason shrugged his wide shoulders. "Didn't figure it was worth a killin', Truman."

Fiona stepped up. "I'll have a glass of bonded sour mash, if you please." She pecked Mason on the cheek. "That's my husband…Always makes me laugh." She grinned as Truman filled a glass for her. "Can't wait to see our children."

Flynn snapped a glance at his wife…

§§§

CHAPTER NINE

BOONS CREEK

"Ow, ow, ow," Bone hollered as he jumped up and shook two hot coals from his smoldering blanket.

Loraine sat cross-legged next to the fire, sipping on a cup of morning coffee. "Told you paybacks were hell, didn't I?"

Bone rubbed his leg and looked up at the red arrows shooting across the gray sky from the east.

"Damn, woman, you coulda burnt me up…and the sun's not even up yet."

"It is somewhere. Coffee's ready…Besides, thought we were going to catch some fish for breakfast."

"Oh, yeah." He stepped over to the fire, still rubbing the hot spot on the side of his leg.

Loraine handed him a tin cup, steaming in the cool morning air.

"Thanks, Pard." He wrapped his huge hands around it, rolling the hot cup back and forth, and then he took a sip. "Hey, not too bad. You may make a camper yet."

Thirty minutes later, Bone handed Loraine her rod and reel. "Here, I put a jitterbug on yours, I'm usin' a tiny torpedo. Both are top waters…Ever used one?"

"A top water lure? Uh, don't think I ever graduated from a worm, bobber and a cane pole."

He chuckled. "Well, this'll be a whole new experience for you…Watch me."

"That's scary to start with," she replied.

"Naw, piece of cake."

He flipped the lure almost to the opposite bank, let it sit in the water for a moment, and then gave the tip of his rod a slight twitch, then another.

The water exploded with a geyser of white as a huge bass hit the lure, careened up in the air, completely out of the water, before splashing back into the creek.

"Hot damn!" He set the hook, lifted the tip of his rod into the air and began reeling the monster fish toward the bank.

"Oh, my goodness, oh, my goodness, you got one," Loraine squealed as she jumped up and down.

Bone worked the fish to the shore, held the rod tip up in the air, reached down, grasped the fish by its lower lip and lifted it out. "Holy cow. Largemouth black bass...gotta weigh four to five pounds."

He unhooked his lure and flipped the fish up higher on the bank. "Okay, Pard, you try it. Just do the same thing I did...Go for it."

Loraine held her rod, twisted her shoulder back and sent the lure flying almost to the middle of the creek. "Didn't go as far as yours...That still..."

She didn't even get a chance to finish her question and to work the lure before it flew up into the air, again, with a tremendous explosion of water and another large bass under it. The lure and fish disappeared with a mighty splash.

"Set the hook, set the hook," yelled Bone.

She gave the tip of the rod a hard jerk, bending the fiberglass shaft almost double.

"Now reel!"

Loraine screamed with every revolution of her handle.

"Keep the tip up," cautioned Bone. "Reel...reel."

She had a much less distance to go than he did, so it was only a few seconds before the big bass was visible under the water, struggling against the tension of the thin monofilament line.

Bone stepped into the edge of the creek, grabbed her line in one hand, the fish's lower lip in the other and lifted it out of the water.

"Wow, this is even bigger than mine...a good seven pounds...Believe we got enough for breakfast, Pard."

"I think I peed my pants," said Loraine as she sat down heavily on the bank.

JACK COUNTY

Lisanne leaned to the side of her red Appaloosa mustang mare with a white blanket on its rear, tracking the wild horse herd, paying particular attention to Steeldust's prints. After two months of tracking the stallion, she could easily pick his hoofprints out from his mares.

"Interestin', Missy, he's takin' his girls in the direction of Wise County...Gonna almost have to cross our place if he keeps headin' that direction."

She squeezed the mare up into an easy rocking chair, mile-eating canter, only occasionally glancing down to make sure she still had his tracks.

She pulled rein on Missy. "What's this?...Shod prints?...Uh, oh, come on girl." Lisanne heeled the game mustang to a gallop just as she heard gunfire.

"Damn!" She urged the mare to an all-out run toward a box canyon a half-mile away. Her long blond hair streamed in the wind behind her as she leaned forward over the horse's neck, encouraging the mustang.

Lisanne could see three men on horseback pushing the herd of wild horses into the narrow neck of a canyon, shooting their pistols in the air.

As they disappeared into the brush at the opening, two of the men dismounted and dragged some cut bushes and saplings across the entrance, effectively blocking it off.

She rode up to the front of the canyon, slipped her Winchester from its boot and jumped from the saddle. "Stay here, I'll be back."

Lisanne's command and leaving the reins loose in front of the mare, ground tied her. She faded into the dense brush.

A mile from the box canyon, Bone and Loraine trotted their horses along a game trail across the grassland, still headed northeast.

Bone reined up. "That's gunfire, Pard."

"Handguns. Sound like .45s."

"Yep...Best we go take a look see. It's not hunters."

"Thought you'd never bring it up."

They heeled their mounts into a hard gallop as several more shots sounded across the rolling prairie grass hills.

"Got a bad feelin' on this," said Bone.

"Me, too."

POLLY'S BOARDING HOUSE

Mason rolled over and kissed Fiona gently on the lips as the first rays of the sun streamed through the windows. "Good mornin' Missus Flynn."

She opened her eyes and kissed him back. "Now I know how Sleeping Beauty must of felt."

"How so." He pecked the tip of her pert nose.

"Being awakened by Prince Charming."

Flynn jumped up and looked around the room. "What? Where is that scoundrel? I'll show him what for."

Fiona giggled and threw her pillow at him. "Mason Flynn! Are you ever serious?" She rolled over and put her feet on the plank floor.

He splashed water in his face from the blue and white ceramic basin. "Not so's you'd notice."

"I suppose you want to go grab some breakfast at Ruth Ann's."

"I could eat a bear...hide, claws an' all."

"Tell me something new."

STEELDUST

He turned toward her after he dried his face on the white towel that came with the room. "Have I told you that I love you?"

"Not yet…today."

He took her face in both of her hands and looked deeply into her steel-gray eyes. "I love you with all my heart, Fiona May Flynn." He kissed her again.

"Lets go eat an' take a ride out toward Lisanne's. Said she was goin' to track down Steeldust an' his girls today."

"I'd like that," Fiona replied.

SHERIFF'S OFFICE

Mason and Fiona strolled along the boardwalk toward Mom's Livery with Newton at their side.

"Guess I better stop in at the office an' tell Gomer to cut those two half-wits loose."

"Bet their heads feel like they've been beat upon."

"Wouldn't be surprised," he said as he opened the door to the office."

Newton headed straight to his spot in front of the potbellied stove and laid down.

"Mornin' Sheriff, Marshal. How was breakfast?"

"Worst I ever had at Ruth Ann's was wonderful," replied Flynn. "How are our guests?"

"Moanin' an' groanin'," Sheriff. "Asked 'em how's come you didn't lock 'em up an' they said you tol' 'em to git in a cell and stay there." Gomer laughed. "Never seen the like."

"Attitude, Deputy, just a little attitude." He walked to the back room to the cells. "Awright, boys, take the pot outside an' dump it in the privy, wash it out an' put it back under the bunks...Pay your five dollar fine to the deputy an' I don't want to see you back here. Understand?...Oh, how're your heads?"

"Feel like it's bigger'n a number two washtub, Sheriff," said the youngest, Archie, glancing at his brother.

Stoner scrunched his eyes and nodded his agreement.

"Maybe you'll learn not to drink so much, next time," said the sheriff.

The brothers nodded again, grabbed their hats, Stoner got the parlor pot an' they headed out the door to the outhouse in the back. A few minutes later, they came back in.

"Pot's clean as a whistle, Sheriff...could even eat out of it," said the youngest, Archie.

"Believe I'll pass...Five dollar fine. Gomer, put it in the special kitty."

Gomer grinned. "Yessir."

The brothers paid their fines, tipped their hats to Fiona.

"Marshal," they said simultaneously as they exited the door.

"Think they'll cut back on their drinks, next time they're in town?" asked Fiona.

"Not likely...least till next payday," replied Flynn. "Gomer, go through that new bunch of dodgers we got in yesterday. See if you spot any familiar faces."

"Yessir...Ya'll goin' out to Lisanne's?"

"Yep, need to see if she's found that stallion."

BOX CANYON

Lisanne crept through the mesquite toward the open center of the canyon. She watched in horror as two of the men hazed Steeldust as the third cast his loop. The rawhide riata settled over the muscular neck of the stallion.

He reared, squealed his rage and charged the man holding the rope, baring his powerful teeth. One of the hazers threw his loop just as the enraged stallion reached his tormentor.

The second roper, dallied off, turned his mount, jerking Steeldust's head from his partner.

The third man also sent his rope over the horse's head, jumped off his own mount and quickly tied the end of his lariat to one of the railroad ties.

The stallion reared high in the air, his front hooves pawing, and screamed his frustrations as the first two ropers quickly loosened their dallies and galloped out of range.

Steeldust lunged about, rearing and bucking at the unfamiliar weight of the eight foot oak railroad tie at the end of the rope about his neck.

Lisanne stepped out of the brush, levering a round into her Winchester. "Let him go!"

"He's ours, missy, we caught him fair an' square," said Carter, the youngest Sinclair as he wheeled his mount around.

"I said let him go." She brought the rifle to her shoulder.

The third cowhand, Fats, off to the far right on her blind side, loosened his second lariat, shook out a loop and flipped it. He dallied off as the noose fell about Lisanne's shoulders and jerked her off her feet causing her to drop the Winchester as she tumbled to the sandy ground. His horse backed up, keeping tension on the rope, like he would a calf. She staggered to her feet and Fats backed his horse again, jerking her back down.

"Now who's got the winnin' hand, you little twit?" said Carter.

Lisanne rolled over to her knees. "You yahoos have gone an peed in your chili, now…You've roped that stallion on my land!"

"And who the hell's ever goin' to know that, split tail?" Carter looked at Fats and Frenchy and laughed malevolently…

§§§

CHAPTER TEN

JACK COUNTY

Mason and Fiona road-trotted their mounts along the trail to Lisanne's Flying L ranch. Fiona's mule was in his patented silk-smooth natural single foot.

They quickly reined up.

"Uh, oh…Gunfire," said Flynn.

"Handguns…Let's ride," commented Fiona.

They squeezed their mounts into a hard gallop in the direction of the shots. It was less than a half a mile to the box canyon.

"The shots came from in there." Flynn pointed to the blocked entrance.

They pulled Laddie and Spot to sliding stops, dismounting as they did. Mason and Fiona, dropped their reins to the sandy soil, ground tying their mounts. They drew their sidearms, automatically separated and disappeared into the scrub brush of mesquite and cedar.

BOX CANYON

Carter dismounted and handed his reins to Frenchy. "Hold these. Fixin' to have me some fun." He strode toward Lisanne, unbuckling his chaps and trousers as he walked.

"You'll regret this," she said as she struggled against the taut rope around her shoulders.

He laughed again. "Not likely...Never regret diddlin' such a sweet young thing."

Carter nodded to Fats who jerked Lisanne to her back in the sand.

Steeldust squealed, reared high in the air and lunged against the heavy green railroad tie he was tied to, dragging it more than ten feet in her direction.

"Assuming you're still able to when we get through with you hoodlums," came a woman's voice from the brush.

The Sinclair hands looked over to see Loraine stepping out from behind a large juniper with her Kimber pointed at Carter in a two-handed grip.

Lisanne rolled over to try to see who was speaking.

"Well, Señorita, you might have the drop on young Carter there, but I got it on you. Now, how's 'bout you drop whatever that is in your hands," said Frenchy from over on Loraine's far left.

He looked over at Fats. "Looks like we're gonna have us a little Mezcan meat to go along with blondie there."

"Not today," came a deep voice from the opposite side of the clearing.

Fats snapped a glance over at Bone stepping out of the brush with his .50 cal pointed at Frenchy.

"Who the hell are you?" asked Fats.

"Well, let's see, the Lone Ranger, John Wayne an' Josey Wales are already taken…so you can just call me, Bone…Sir."

"Haw, I'd say we got us a Mezcan standoff…to coin a phrase," said Frenchy.

"Like the big man said, 'Not today'." Flynn held his .45 Colt at waist level as he stepped out in the open.

"I'm getting real tired of seeing you boys. This is twice in the last two days…Now drop 'em," said Fiona with an Ivory-handled .38-40 Peacemaker in each hand as she followed Mason out of the cedars to his far right. "You're all under arrest."

"I'd do what the Marshal says, girls, she's as good with one hand as the other an' can shoot in two directions at the same time…Plus man mountain over there is holdin' the biggest handgun I've ever seen and your boss is standin' there with his pants unbuttoned."

Bone glanced over at Loraine. "Say, have we killed anybody today, Pard?"

"Not yet."

"Well, hell, somebody's got to be first." He thumbed the hammer back ominously on his big

Smith and Wesson 500 and pointed it at the youngest Sinclair.

"Hey, hey, hey, wait a minute, wait a minute," whined Carter.

Fiona grinned at Bone's comment, and then asked, "You all right, Lisanne?"

She struggled to her feet again and slipped the lariat back over her head and glared at Fats. "Am now...Who's got a foldin' knife?"

Bone unclipped his 3.5 inch black Benchmade 154CM knife from his web belt and pitched it to her.

Lisanne easily caught it in the air and stared at it for a moment, turning it over in her hand. "Awright, I give, how do you open it?"

"Silver button on the end...press it an' keep your fingers off the blade side."

She pushed the small knurled steel button and the three and a half inch blade sprung into the open and locked position. "Oh! My goodness," Lisanne said as she jumped.

Be careful, you can shave with that thing...uh, well at least I can."

"Perfect...Exactly what I need."

She turned toward the tense, quivering stallion, taking very slow and short steps while softly humming, holding the knife against her leg. He blew loudly through his nostrils and pawed the sand.

Lisanne started to make little kissing sounds. Steeldust perked up his ears at the interesting noise. She took a few more steps. He snorted again, but softer.

"Hello, boy, you know me…I won't hurt you," she said in almost a whisper and made more kissing noises.

Lisanne slowly held out her left hand, palm facing the ground, and with her fingers curled in. The stallion reached out his muzzle and sniffed of the back of her fingers as she softly caressed the velvet hair between his nostrils.

He wiggled his upper lip over her fingers. All the time she kept making the quiet kissing noises with her lips.

"It's awright, big boy. I'm goin' to help you." She continued the soft humming of a seventeenth century folk song, *Lavender's Blue*, as she slid her hand up between his eyes with a gentle stroking motion. His big, soft, brown eyes closed slightly in pleasure as he lowered his head.

Lisanne moved her left hand down to the first loose loop and easily slipped it over his head.

"Easy now, we're goin' to get these nasty old ropes off of you," she said sotto voce as she reached slowly down to the second noose and eased it over his head and off his nose also. He blew softly.

Lisanne paused and started singing *Lavender's Blue* just under her breath, *"Lavender's blue, dilly dilly, Lavender's green, When you are king, dilly dilly, I shall be queen…"*

Steeldust's eyes again drooped at her melodious and calming voice as she reached for the rawhide honda around his neck with it still attached to the heavy tie, thirty-five feet away.

She pressed her cheek lovingly against the wild stallion's jaw as she slowly moved her right hand with the knife toward the lariat.

"Hey, you cain't do that! We catched him fair and square," yelled Carter.

"Like she said, buttercup, you roped that stallion on her land," said Loraine. "That's trespassing where we come from."

"And I suggest you button your lip before you find my fist in your mouth." Bone held up his ham-like left hand and grinned. "You won't like it...trust me."

"You can't threaten me," said Carter as he buttoned up his pants.

"Oh, I don't threaten, sweet-cheeks...I make guarantees...that you can carve in stone."

Steeldust had jerked his head up at the crass sound of Carter's voice.

Lisanne patiently started over with her hand caressing his forehead and continued the song, *"...Who told you so, dilly dilly, Who told you so? 'Twas my own heart, dilly dilly, That told me so'..."*

She pressed the edge of Bone's knife at a slight angle against the tough rawhide as she held the honda with her left. The tension of the rope allowed the razor sharp blade to virtually slice through the braided riata with ease.

Steeldust jerked his head again at the release of the pressure as the rawhide rope parted.

Lisanne eased the last noose over his nose. "There all gone...Feel better?"

She whispered more words in his ear as she stroked the side of his neck with her left hand, hiding the knife beside her leg again.

He snorted softly and nuzzled the side of her face.

"Now go. Go to your ladies…We'll talk again later."

The magnificent steeldust stallion squealed, rolled back over his heels and galloped toward his herd of mares.

"You did it, Lisanne, you touched him…He'll never forget it," said Flynn.

"That was beautiful," added Fiona.

"I never seen anythin' like it," commented Bone, you're a real live horse whisperer."

Lisanne glanced at him and handed his knife back. "Whatever that is."

"A person who can communicate with horses on a spiritual level. My Padrino can do that," answered Bone as he pressed the button, closed the blade and clipped it back to his belt.

"This ain't over, by a long shot. I'm still gonna git that bastard," said Carter.

"Not for a while, you're not," said Flynn.

"Oh? How so?"

"Because you're goin' to be in my hoosegow."

"On what charge?" demanded Carter.

"Well, like the lady…" He looked over. "Loraine, isn't it?"

"Yes, but how did you know?" she replied, furrowing her brow.

"We'll get to that later." He turned back to Carter. "…Like Loraine said, trespassin' to start. And I think ropin' this young girl an' jerkin' her down to the ground constitutes aggravated assault…Right, officer Bone?"

"Uh…right. I'd say so, Sheriff…"

"Flynn, Mason Flynn and this is my wife, Deputy US Marshal Fiona Mae Flynn, formerly Miller."

"Oh, my gosh," Bone muttered under his breath, and then added, "Got any laws around here on animal cruelty?"

"Might take a while to look it up while we have them incarcerated," said Flynn.

"My daddy ain't gonna put up with this," Carter yelled.

"Your daddy ain't gonna have no say, squirt, leastwise till the judge sets your bail…in a week or two when he comes back through town," said Flynn

"You cain't do this!"

"Watch us," said Fiona. "Now, you other nimrods get off those horses." She nodded at Flynn and they each pulled out a set of cuffs. "Looks like we're short a pair of manacles…"

"Wouldn't say that, Marshal," Bone pulled out a set of chrome-plated cuffs from his cargo pocket and walked over to Carter. "Hands behind your back…" He glanced over at Flynn and grinned. "…squirt."

Bone pulled the young man's arms back and expertly snapped the cuffs on.

"Ow, ow, that's too tight," complained Carter.

"The sheriff can loosen 'em if he wants to." Bone pitched him the key.

"When we get to town," said Flynn as he snatched the key out of the air, and then snapped his manacles around Fat's wrists, also behind him. "Purty good idea there, Bone, putting their hands behind their backs."

"Always worked for us…Helps keep 'em out of mischief…Right, Pard?"

"Tends to discourage any shenanigans."

"Or a shenanigan," added Bone.

"How we gonna hold on to the saddle?" asked Frenchy.

"I'd suggest you stay in the middle...any horseman can do that...right Lisanne?"

"Should, Fiona...depends on how well they've trained their mounts, though." She grinned. "Wonder how many times ya'll are gonna have to stop an' pick them up outta the road?"

"You gotta start all over now that you let Steeldust go?" inquired Mason.

Lisanne shook her head. "Don't think so...We talked. He's not goin' to take his girls far...Got plenty water and grass."

"You talked?" asked Fiona.

She looked over at the raven-haired beauty, winked and grinned. "Uh, huh."

§§§

CHAPTER ELEVEN

BOX CANYON

Bone helped Flynn put a sullen Carter, Fats and Big Jim French into their saddles outside the mouth of the canyon.

"By, the way, Bone, where are ya'll from? I know you're cops."

"Don't think you'd believe me if I told you, Sheriff."

"You might be surprised…An' where'd you get those side arms? That .50 cal is somethin' else…not to say anythin' about that semiautomatic of Loraine's…Seen a picture of one made in Germany in the Police Gazette…but it didn't look nothin' like hers."

"Yeah, I know…'Fraid that falls into the same category as where we're from."

"We need to talk," said Fiona. "Why don't ya'll go ahead and ride into Jacksboro with us. We can visit after we get these malefactors behind bars."

"Well, like to, but we're kinda headed in the opposite direction…Right, Pard?"

"So you say, Bone," replied Loraine.

"Where'bouts?" asked Flynn.

"Lookin' for the Wilson ranch. It's to the northeast from here."

Mason's head snapped around from tying the leads of the prisoner's mounts in a daisy chain. "Whose ranch?"

"The Wilsons."

"Cletus and Mary Lou?"

"Yeah, think that's it. Got…uh, a daughter, Lucy?"

Flynn grinned. "Uh, huh…Mary Lou's my sister."

"Oh, really?"

"How do you know them?" asked Flynn.

"Well, don't really know Cletus and your sis, but, again, that's part of that thing you wouldn't believe." Bone glanced over at the prisoners.

Flynn caught his look and for the first time, noticed the gold and turquoise bracelet peeking out from Bone's sleeve. "Ah, get your point…Notice you failed to include Lucy…"

"Uh…well, yeah." Bone looked at Loraine and pulled his sleeve back down.

"Tell you what do, ya'll go ahead and come to Jacksboro with us so we can lock these lawbreakers up an' we'll have us a long chat…an' maybe some lunch at the best restaurant north of Fort Worth…Then me an' Fiona will take ya'll to my sister's an' interduce you proper."

"Wish I could go, too. Like to meet your sister an' her family, but Slim an' I got a new hired hand we're breakin' in," said Lisanne.

"A new hired hand? Where'd he come from?" asked Fiona.

"Caught him stealin' meat from my smokehouse."

"An' you hired him?" inquired an incredulous Flynn.

"Yeah, long story." She also cast a hard look at the prisoners.

"Whew, there's a whole lot we don't know that we need to catch up on," said the sheriff.

"You don't know the half of it…Why don't ya'll stop by on the way to the Wilsons. Fill you in…Think you and Fiona will be interested."

"Well, like I always say…When you don't know that you don't know…it's a whole lot different than when you know that you don't know…until you know it," commented Bone.

"What?" quipped Flynn.

"Explain later, Dear," said Fiona.

"I'll be interested in hearing that too, Marshal," commented Loraine as she looked out of the corner of her eye at Bone.

He just looked back at her arched his eyebrows and grinned.

"Is he like this all the time, Loraine?" asked Flynn.

She nodded. "Pretty much."

The sheriff shook his head, stuck his boot in Laddie's stirrup and swung into the saddle. "Let's head 'em out, folks…Only 'bout five miles to town."

"See ya'll later," said Lisanne as she also mounted her Appaloosa.

"When you gonna try for Steeldust again?" asked Fiona.

"Told him I'd give him a few days to get his ladies an' himself settled down after those idiots chased 'em into this canyon, shootin' their guns."

"He said alright?" asked Bone.

"Uh, huh," she replied with a grin.

"Huh…Just like my Padrino."

"Who's Padrino?" inquired Flynn.

"My godfather."

JACKSBORO, TEXAS

Rowdy Sinclair stepped out of the Coolwater Saloon, stopped next to a canopy post, pulled out his makings from his vest pocket and rolled a quirly. As he struck a match on the post and lit the roll-your-own, he looked up to see the sheriff, the marshal, a giant of a man, and another woman rein up in front of the jail. Flynn was leading his little brother, Fats, and Frenchy—all three were shackled.

"Son of a bitch," the tall, lanky, number two Sinclair hissed as he shook the match and pitched it in the street.

He waited until the sheriff led the prisoners inside his office, stepped down and untied his blood bay gelding from the hitchrail. Rowdy took one last draw of his cigarette and pitched it to the dirt. He stabbed his toe in his steel oxbow stirrup and forked his saddle.

"Daddy's gonna have a hissy-fit," he muttered as he spurred his horse into a gallop out of town, back toward the Bar S.

Deputy Platt jumped to his feet as the group entered the sheriff's office.

"Well, looky here, we got us some new residents." He glanced at the three men with their hands shackled behind their backs.

"Gomer, let's put these two in one cell an' baby Sinclair here in another," said Flynn.

"I ain't no baby," he shouted back.

"Then you shouldn't act like one," commented Fiona.

Gomer opened one of the three cells on the left side of the hall as Flynn marched Carter inside. He reached in his shirt pocket for the key Bone had given him and unshackled him.

Sinclair rubbed both wrists vigorously and held them up to show Flynn. "See? Looky at them red marks. Tol' you they's too tight."

"You'll get over it," said Flynn as he closed the cell door behind him and nodded to Gomer to lock it.

He stepped across the hall as Bone ushered the other two inside the only empty cell on the other side of the hall. They turned around to allow him to unlock their iron shackles.

"Have a seat, girls," the sheriff said as he handed Bone his cuffs and key back.

"You just wait till my daddy hears about this…he'll show ya'll what for," said Carter.

"Can't wait," commented Bone as he stepped back into the office area.

Flynn opened one of the drawers of his desk and pulled out a pad of papers. "Here, Deputy Platt, need to fill out the charges for these yahoos."

"What are they, Sheriff?"

"Well, trespassin' to start, larceny of horses and top it off with aggravated assault." He turned back to the cell area. "That little girl is underage, boys, in case you didn't know…an' we'll see as we can find anything on cruelty to animals to add to it."

"Now there you go, Sheriff, didn't know Lisanne was underage," said Bone.

"That should put the icing on the cake," added Loraine.

"I'd say," replied Flynn. He turned to the deputy again. "We're goin' down to Ruth Ann's an' see if she's got any of the special left…Might be all gone since it's purtnear two o'clock."

Gomer grinned. "Bet not. Ain't never seen her run out…It's pot roast today an' dewberry cobbler."

Newton bounced up and down on his front feet and woofed.

"Do love dewberry cobbler," commented Bone.

Platt looked at the big man and Loraine, and then back at Flynn with a questioning expression on his face.

"Oh, Deputy, this is Detective D.U. Bone an' Inspector Loraine Rodriguez, they're uh…visitin' law officers."

"How do, Inspector…Detective."

"It's just Bone and Loraine, Deputy Platt."

"Yessir."

"And Sir was my daddy," replied Bone.

"Uh…yes…uh, Bone." Gomer shyly grinned.

"Keep the door locked an' don't let anybody in you don't know…Got it? We're goin' to take our mounts down to Mom's an' then go eat."

BAR S RANCH

Rowdy pulled his jaded and lathered gelding to a stumbling stop in front of the porch of the rambling ranch house.

He jumped from the saddle and sprinted up the steps to the door as his exhausted horse, his flanks heaving, stood where he had stopped.

"Pa! Pa! Come quick."

The Sinclair patriarch pushed open the door with his left hand while his right held his ubiquitous glass of scotch.

"What the Sam Hill you yellin' about, boy?"

"It's Carter, Pa. The sheriff done locked him, Fats, and Frenchy up in the jail house."

STEELDUST

"Son of a bitch…When?"

"'Bout thirty minutes ago. Rode here quick as I could."

Sinclair glanced at the lathered and winded gelding in front of the porch. "So, I see…Saddle my horse, get a fresh one for yourself, then find your brother and some of the other boys and mount up."

"What are we gonna do, Pa?"

"Go to town and get your brother out of jail, you idiot." He spun on his heels and went back in the house to get his gunbelt.

Ten minutes later, Algernon Sinclair, III and his men galloped out of the front gate toward Jacksboro.

MOM'S LIVERY

"Who do these other three horses belong to, Sheriff," asked Mom as her son, Haircut, led them to the side corral.

"Carter Sinclair and two of their gunhawks," said Flynn.

"Uh, oh. I smell trouble comin'…Say, who's this big feller here." She nodded at Bone.

"Uh, well, he's called Bone and that's his partner, Loraine…They're…uh, peace officers from out of town," replied Fiona.

"You go duck huntin' with a rake, do ya?" she asked Bone, looking up at his 6'8" height.

"Only if I can't find a hoe." Bone grinned.

"I can believe it." Mom grinned back at him. "I'll lock your long guns in the office…No need in carryin' 'em around."

"Thanks, Mom," replied Loraine.

SEWEL'S CAFE

Flynn, Fiona, Bone and Loraine sat at a round table in the far corner of the dinning room. There were only four other customers remaining from lunch scattered about.

Emma Lou walked up to their table with a large wicker picnic basket and interrupted their conversation. "I'm goin' ahead an' take the prisoners some lunch, if that's all right, Sheriff…Gomer's already eaten."

"Fine, Emma Lou, thanks," he responded.

Keeping his voice low, Flynn continued after she left, "Well, if we didn't already know Lucy an' her story…" He glanced at Fiona. "We might have difficulty believin' ya'll's…but, that's not the case."

"The fact that you have an identical bracelet to the one she wears and we know some of the things it can do…seals the deal," said Fiona. "The fact that H.G. Wells published *The Time Machine* in 1895 and Mark Twain, *A Connecticut Yankee in King Author's Court* in 1889, shows that time travel is possible…at least in their imaginations."

"And knowin' that *Annuna*, or Lucy, is from another world doesn't make it that hard to believe…does it?" asked Bone.

"Don't forget the other alien race, the enemies of the *Anunnaki*…the Reptoids," said Loraine.

"Yeah, my pard and I shot down one of their ball type crafts as it was taking off."

"With your .50 an' her semiautomatic?" asked Flynn.

"Yup."

"I can believe it." Flynn handed a patiently waiting Newton a scrap of pot roast fat from his plate.

"Do you think she can help you get back to your time?" asked Fiona.

"No idea. It's just a wild shot...Hell, we're not even sure how we got here."

"The shaman of the Chickasaw tribe across the Red, *Anompoli Lawa,* showed us one of those spiral petroglyphs beside a cave up in the Nations a few months ago...He said it was a conduit for a demon to another dimension or something," said Fiona.

Down the street, Sinclair and his hands drew rein in front of the jail and dismounted.

"Harley, go down to Mom's Livery. I saw Carter's and the other horses in the corral...Bring 'em up here."

He, Rowdy, Al, and two of the other gunhands stepped up to the door. Gomer had failed to re-lock it after he let Emma Lou in with the lunches.

Platt got to his feet as the men strode through the door. "Say, ya'll ain't allowed in here."

"You don't say," said Rowdy.

STEELDUST

"Unlock them cells in the back," said Algernon Sinclair.

"Cain't do that," said Gomer.

"I said unlock 'em," he backhanded Platt across the mouth, splitting his lip.

Emma Lou screamed as Gomer's blood splattered her face.

Al hit her on the side of her head with his fist, knocking her to the floor, out cold.

"Damn you!" Gomer lunged at the oldest Sinclair only to have Rowdy and Baker each grab an arm.

"Hold him," said the patriarch as he slipped on his black doeskin gloves and commenced to pummel the young man with both fists repeatedly, first in the face and then to his midsection and ribs and then back to the face with powerful sledgehammer blows.

"Let him go," he finally said. "I'm tired of beating on him."

The two men unceremoniously dropped Gomer, unconscious, to the plank floor like a pile of wet newspaper.

"That ought to teach the snot-nosed kid he can't smart mouth a Sinclair an' get away with it," commented Rowdy.

Gomer was bleeding profusely from his nose and mouth. Both of his eyes were swollen completely shut and already turning black...

§§§

CHAPTER TWELVE

SEWEL'S CAFE

Flynn led the way out the nine foot glass-centered front door, ringing the three inch brass bell attached to the header. He held the door for the others and shut it when they were all standing on the boardwalk. Newton sat down beside Fiona's foot.

Bone looked down the street to the sheriff's office on the opposite side. "Say, Sheriff, didn't you tell Gomer to keep the door shut?"

Flynn, glance down at his office to see the door standing wide open. "Oh, damnation."

He took off at a dead run, followed by Bone and the others. "Honey, go down the other way an' get Doc Mosier…Got a bad feelin'," he said to his wife.

Fiona spun around and headed toward the doctor's office in the next block.

Bone's long legs quickly outdistanced the sheriff's. He reached the door, drew his S&W 500, stepped inside, and quickly looked around. "Clear."

He had noticed Gomer and Emma Lou on the floor, and then the open two-inch thick door to the cells in the back.

"Son of a bitch," he exclaimed. "They let all the prisoners out." Bone knelt beside Gomer and felt his neck for a pulse. "Damn."

Flynn burst into the room, with Newton, followed by a breathless Loraine. He stopped beside Bone.

"Is he…"

"Barely," he said glancing up. "Where's that doc?"

"Comin'…Aw, Hell and the devil, they let Wild Bob an' his gang, out, too," said Flynn as he looked through the open door to the back room at the empty cells.

Loraine knelt beside Emma Lou and checked her pulse. "She's got a strong beat…With this bruise on her cheek I'd say was from somebody's fist…she's knocked out, probably concussed." She started patting her hand and caressing the side of her face. "Wake up, Emma."

Fiona led a fast-walking sixty-eight year old Doctor Curtis Mosier, carrying his black valise, in the door. The thin, white-haired physician quickly assessed the situation.

He handed Loraine a vial of salts, and then knelt by Gomer. The doctor took out his stethoscope and checked Platt's heartbeat, lung sounds, depth of his breathing and then pulled his shirt open and palpated his blackening ribs and bruised abdominal area. Finally he lifted one of Gomer's eyelids and passed his hand in front of his eye, temporarily blocking the light, and then removed it.

He shook his head, grimaced and looked up at Flynn. "Like to have beat the boy to death."

"He gonna make it?"

The doctor frowned. "Can't tell yet...Broken nose, two, maybe three broken ribs...don't think any of them punctured his lungs, though...multiple deep tissue contusions and a severe concussion...Could have internal bleeding, can't tell yet."

Mosier started wiping the blood from the deputy's face. "I've seen men stomped by a horse or bull not busted up this bad."

"Think they tried to kill him?" asked Bone.

The doctor looked at him questioningly, and then at Flynn.

"This is Detective Darrell Ulysses Bone, Doc, an' that's his partner, Inspector Loraine Rodriquez...They're, uh...from out of town."

Mosier nodded, and then replied, "Well, to answer that question requires an opinion and mine is...yes."

Bone glanced over at Flynn and then at Fiona. "Probably didn't want to fire a shot. Bring unwanted attention before they made their getaway."

STEELDUST

He looked at Loraine. "Looks like we're gonna have to put off goin' up to see Lucy, Pard...We got work to do, a 10-98...Amazin' how the more things change, the more they stay the same."

"What's a 10-98?" asked Flynn

"We code things by number back home. A 10-98 means a felonious jail break...with injuries."

"Why don't you just say that?" commented Flynn.

"Thought I did...I don't tolerate men gangin' up on a boy and I damn sure don't tolerate somebody hittin' a woman...of any age." His gold-flecked amber eyes looked hard at Flynn, and then Fiona. "I get 'em first."

JACK COUNTY
FLYING L RANCH

"Slim, why don't you go huntin' an' see as you can scare up some game for supper? Some fresh venison would be nice," said Lisanne.

"By the Lord Jim, missy, that sounds good. Seen some fresh sign when we wuz down to the creek.

Let me fetch my Sharps," said the Chickasaw Freedman.

"Gonna show Buster how to warm up one of the green mustangs in the round pen...That strawberry roan long filly...I like her."

"I'm workin' with a horse already?" Buster asked.

"Just enough so's you're not scared of 'em...They can sense your fear an' they'll run all over you when they do...You're just gonna watch today, though."

"Horses is herd animals, son...They always lookin' fer a leader...'less they already be one," said Slim as he headed for the bunkhouse to get his rifle.

"You be the leader or they will...end of story," she said.

Buster looked out at the seventy-foot diameter round pen made of mostly vertical six foot cedar posts on two inch spacing, held together by three strands of number twelve slick wire.

"How come the pen is round?"

"Don't want to give 'em a corner they think they can get trapped in...They'll panic."

"Oh." Buster nodded his head.

Lisanne reached back, pulled her long blond hair around to the side, braided it into a single thick braid and let it drape over her left shoulder.

She and Buster waved as Slim trotted out of the barn on his grulla gelding and headed toward the creek bottom.

"Good luck," yelled Lisanne.

He touched the brim of his beat-up gray slouch hat and nodded.

Lisanne leaned her twelve gauge against the outside of the pen, opened the narrow horse gate, and led the way inside. She carried a coiled hemp lariat in one hand.

The young strawberry roan long filly stood in the center, her eyes focused on Lisanne, muscles quivering.

She turned to Buster. "Now you stay behind me an' watch…Don't make any sudden moves, like scratchin' your nose…or other parts."

He nodded.

Lisanne began slowly twirling the knotted end of the rope in a lazy circle to the side and humming a tune. The filly watched the knot go around and around until she flicked it in the direction of the horse's rear.

The roan turned, ran to the side of the pen and starting galloping around the inside away from the rope as Lisanne and Buster moved to the center.

Lisanne stayed on the filly's rear quarter, still slowly twirling the rope. Then she stepped toward the horse's shoulder and flicked the knot in front of her.

The roan slid to a stop, whirled about and headed in the opposite direction—not as fast this time. Her gallop slowed to a lope with a natural inside lead, and then to a trot as Lisanne reversed her several more times.

Finally she laid the coiled lariat on the ground by her feet and softly said, "Whoa…whoa, girl…Easy now."

She squatted down—Buster followed her lead.

The filly slowed her trot to a walk, finally stopped, turned, faced the pair and blew her nostrils as Lisanne continued to softly talk to her.

After she stopped, the filly took a couple of hesitant steps toward the two teenagers, and then a couple more.

"Come on girl, come to me." She held out her left hand with her palm to the ground, her fingers curled and made those soft kissing sounds like with Steeldust.

Lisanne turned her head a little to Buster. "Don't move a muscle." She turned back to the filly. "Come on…"

The roan filly tentatively reached out her muzzle to Lisanne's curled fingers and sniffed.

"That's a good girl…" She purred as she rubbed the horse's forehead with her other hand, further calming the wild animal.

Lisanne slowly stood and turned back to Buster. "See, it doesn't take snubbin' a horse to a post, blindfoldin' it, jumpin' in the saddle, and spurrin' the bejesus outta 'em…The Comanche, Cheyenne an' Kiowa are considered the greatest light cavalry in the world…Ever seen a Injun wearin' spurs?"

"Uh…Well, cain't say as I have."

"An' you won't. This is the way they train a horse to ride…not by buckin' 'em down an' breakin' their spirit…"

Three miles west out of Jacksboro, Algernon Sinclair, III, raised his hand for the group of riders to stop. He turned to Wild Bob.

"All right, you and your men head south for the Brazos here."

Bob glanced at his men. He was holding his bandaged, maimed hand against his chest. It was obviously still painful.

"Uh, don't you think we'd be better off stickin' together?"

"I didn't ask for your damn opinion, fool, I told you to head south…Got that?"

"Yessir," replied Bob. He squinted his eyes at Sinclair. "Usin' us to distract the sheriff, ain'tcha?"

"Maybe you're not as dumb as you look…Coulda left your sorry asses in Flynn's jail…At least now you got a chance of avoidin' a hemp necktie."

"What about our guns?"

Sinclair looked over at Baker. "Give 'em their gunbelts, Cullen…It's a good thing your horses were at the livery or ya'll might be walking."

Sinclair's gunhawk handed over the belts to the four men.

Wild Bob looped his over his saddlehorn as his hand wouldn't allow him to buckle it about his waist. "How 'bout our long guns?"

"We didn't get them…but give 'em that Henry," he said to Baker.

"Just one?" questioned one of Bob's men.

"Consider yourself lucky to get that. You boys broke the law, you belong in jail, so count your blessin's." He grinned wryly. "Now, haul your carcasses outta here." Sinclair drew his Colt, thumbed back the hammer and pointed it at Wild Bob's forehead. "Want me to say it again?"

The outlaw leader ground his teeth together and turned his horse toward the south. "Let's go, boys," he said as he glared back at Sinclair.

They trotted off over the rolling north central Texas grassland.

"Now where, Pa?" asked Carter.

"Now we go get that little split-tail and make her catch that stallion for us."

"What about the sheriff, his wife an' them strangers Carter mentioned?" asked Rowdy.

"They'll split up. That's why I sent those outlaws in another direction…Some'll head south, rest after us…We'll settle their hash then cut for our mountain place in northern New Mexico…with the girl and that steeldust stallion," said Sinclair.

§§§

CHAPTER THIRTEEN

SHERIFF'S OFFICE
JACKSBORO, TEXAS

"Sheriff! Sheriff," yelled Bert Mayfield, a local ranch hand, as he burst through the still open doorway.

Flynn looked up from where he was kneeling next to Doc Mosier tending to Gomer. "What is it, Bert?"

"It's Mom an' her boy, Haircut!…Somebody pistol whipped the both of 'em." He glanced over at the doctor. "Might oughta go down there, Doc."

"Are they unconscious?" asked Mosier without looking up.

"No sir, they're sittin' up in the middle of the aisleway, kindly confused…bleedin' a mite bit from where they was hit on the head."

"Go back down there and make sure they don't get up and move around till I get there…Understand?" ordered Mosier.

"Yessir." Bert spun on his heel and headed back down to Mom's Livery.

"You going to leave the town without any law?" asked Loraine.

Flynn shook his head. "We'll go out to Lisanne's an' deputize Slim…He used to be one of my deputies before goin' to work out at the Flyin' L… Plus there's the town marshal…Purty well useless as tits on a boar hog, but, he and his deputy will be a presence."

"Need to see about gettin' some of your spare guns…Only have twenty rounds plus the five in the wheel for my .50," commented Bone.

"Same goes for me," said Loraine. "Got three magazines."

"Isn't your semiautomatic a .45?" replied Flynn.

"Yes, but your ammo is black powder. These use a new smokeless powder...Not sure it'll work in my Kimber," she added.

"Ah, heard about that stuff. The military has started using it, but it's not available to the public yet," said Fiona.

"It should work, Pard, just have to clean your .45 more often on account that black powder leaves a hellova lot more residue and the power is not quite the same," commented Bone. "I'm goin' to carry a .45 Peacemaker an' save my 500 for backup."

"Well, one of your rare good ideas, Bone."

"You'll think good ideas, Pard..."

Loraine turned to Flynn. "You got any extra revolvers in your cabinet?"

"Think I can handle that. Sinclair only got his boy's handguns and rifles along with Wild Bob's...I keep others from previous cases in my safe over in the corner. Got Colts, Remingtons and S&Ws." Flynn nodded toward the three foot square iron box.

"Loraine's got a later model '66 Yellowboy an' I got a '86 Winchester .45-70 Government center-fire we took from Wild Bob's horses. Left 'em down at Mom's, back in her office," said Bone.

"Chances are they're still there. Doubt they took the time to go through her office," said Flynn. "But, if they did, got some locked up...plus plenty ammo."

Emma Lou was sitting up while Loraine held a cool damp cloth against the side of her cheek when Deputy Platt gave out with a soft moan.

"Gomer," she exclaimed as she tried to get up, but was stopped by Loraine.

"You stay put for a bit, Emma."

"Looks like the boy is starting to come around...that's a good sign," said Doc Mosier.

His eyes flickered as he tried to see through the swelling. "Cain't see."

Mosier laid a cool, damp cloth over his eyes. "Don't try, Gomer...Your eyes are swollen completely shut. Just relax and breathe softly."

"Unggg...cain't do that either," he wheezed and then moaned at the pain.

"I need a couple of litters from my office." The doctor glanced over at Fiona.

"I'll go get them…You want to give me a hand, Loraine?" She got to her feet and turned to Emma. "You stay put, all right?"

The teenager held the cool rag against the bruise on the side of her face and nodded. It was obvious she was still a bit groggy.

"Stop by the Coolwater, hon, an' recruit four cowboys or locals to help." Flynn looked at the doctor. "I'm assumin' you want them both carried down to your office," said Flynn.

"I do…Need to watch them both for at least twenty-four hours."

"Who was it that worked you over, Gomer?" asked Flynn.

He groaned, "Unnn, old man Sinclair…Rowdy an'…an' one of…one of his hired hands…Baker…I think it was…held my arms."

"That's enough talking for now, Gomer," said Doctor Mosier. "We're going to move you and Emma down to my clinic."

He nodded and whispered, "Been there before."

Ten minutes later, Fiona, Loraine, and four men from the saloon entered the sheriff's office with two military style litters.

Two of the men, a merchant and a cowhand, laid one of the canvas stretchers beside Gomer. Flynn and Bone gently lifted the deputy to the center amidst his moans of pain.

"Ya'll be particular with him, now," said Doctor Mosier. "My nurse, Gertrude, will show you where to put him when you get to my clinic." He turned to the other cowboys standing beside Emma. "Same for you gentlemen."

Bone and Flynn eased her onto the litter for the other two men. The sheriff squeezed Emma's hand and gave her a supporting nod as they carried her out of the door following Gomer.

Flynn glanced at the others. "Well, we need to go to Barber's Mercantile an' get some trail supplies after we go down to Mom's with the Doc."

"Might as well get those handguns before we leave, don't you think Sheriff?" asked Bone.

"Yep," he replied as he stepped over to the safe, squatted down and spun the dial.

After swinging the thick door open, he reached in and grabbed two gunbelts. One was a SAA .45 and the other was a .44-40.

"You got the '66, right, Loraine?"
She nodded.

He handed her the .44-40. "Takes the same ammo as the Yellowboy. Got a leather punch if the belt is too big…which it looks like it is." Flynn grinned. "You an' Fiona have wasp waists."

"May have to let it out, though if she buckles it around her hips."

"Damn you, Bone, I'm going to kill you," Loraine replied as she wheeled around and looked for something to throw at him.

"You sure ya'll aren't married?" asked Fiona.

Bone and Loraine simultaneously replied, "Not in this lifetime."

MOM'S LIVERY

Flynn led the group of law officers and Doctor Mosier into the alleyway of the livery barn with Newton padding alongside. Mom and her son were sitting in the scattered oat straw.

Bert and several other townsfolk including Ruth Ann from the Sewel's down the street were attending the pair with damp cloths to their heads—the blood had been wiped away.

"Bring those chairs over here, boys," ordered Mosier. "Let's get 'em off the floor."

Several of the town's citizens grabbed the two slat-backed chairs outside Mom's office and brought them to the doctor.

He assisted Mom and her son into the chairs and checked their eyes and pulse.

"How do you feel, Mom?" he asked.

"Like I been hit over the head, Curtis, what the hell do you think?"

He held up two fingers. "How many fingers do you see?"

"I see two, you old fool," she growled.

"Any dizziness?"

"No…Just a headache."

Mosier repeated the same with Haircut with identical results.

He handed Mom a small green vial. "Here's some laudanum for the pain…Some willow bark tea will help, also. "Ya'll were lucky. Just take it easy for a couple of days."

"Got work to do, Doc." She looked at Mason. "What all did they git, Sheriff?"

"Looks like just their and Wild Bob's horses. Haven't looked in your office yet."

Mom glanced at the padlock on the door to her small office. "Still locked. Didn't get the guns or your an' Fiona's custom saddles."

"That's a good thing…Do you have some horses for Loraine and man mountain here? We're goin' after 'em."

"Got a seventeen hand chestnut part Friesian in the back trap that should suit him just fine…There's a lineback dun mare back there, too, for Loraine."

Flynn turned to Fiona. "We'll saddle up if ya'll will go down to Barber's for those supplies."

She nodded and pecked him on the cheek. "We can do that, right Loraine?"

"Waiting on you."

FLYING L RANCH

"See?" Lisanne ran her hands up and down the roan filly's legs. "You get 'em used to your touch an' voice…lettin' 'em know you're not goin' to hurt 'em. Horses are prey animals…their first instinct is to run an' second is they'll fight. Can take a plug outta you in a heartbeat."

"Can I try that?" Buster asked.

"Sure." She backed away and let him touch the filly.

"They will always respond to love an' affect…"

The two turned at the sound of galloping hoof beats coming from back of the barn.

The startled filly snorted, spun and ran to the side of the pen as Sinclair and his men charged around the corner.

Buster sprinted toward the cedar post wall and the shotgun leaning against the outside. The young man reached the top and vaulted over.

A pistol shot rang out. He crumpled like a shot dove in flight and tumbled the six feet to the ground on the outside of the round pen with a thud. Buster laid there, limp as a rag doll.

"Buster!" Lisanne screamed and ran toward the narrow gate.

"Hold it right there, missy," said Rowdy as he pointed his still smoking Colt in her direction.

The patriarch leaned forward and crossed his arms over his saddlehorn. "You're comin' with us, little lady." He glanced around. "Where's the nigger?"

"He's, uh, gone huntin'...be back most anytime."

"No matter. We're not going to be here long," said Sinclair.

The youngest, Carter, dismounted, opened the gate and stepped inside with a malevolent grin on his face. He grabbed her by the arm and dragged her out.

Lisanne glanced at the unmoving form of the young man lying at the bottom of the wall. "But, Buster..."

Rowdy followed her gaze. "Wouldn't worry 'bout him. I don't miss...Kid's dead."

§§§

CHAPTER FOURTEEN

JACK COUNTY, TEXAS

Flynn and Fiona led the group west out of town straight toward Lisanne's ranch. They reached the entrance gate of the Flying L at the same time Slim was returning from his hunt.

"Slim," yelled Mason as they rode closer.

The former deputy had a six point buck draped over the back of his horse.

"Sheriff, Fiona, how ya'll are?...Who's yer friends?"

"This is Detective Bone and his partner, Inspector Loraine Rodriguez. They're law officers...uh, from out of town."

"How do?" He looked at Bone. "Dang, feller, you could go bear huntin' with a switch."

"Naw, not really...Usually use a baseball bat." Bone grinned.

"Haw, you say...Looks like ya'll are supplied up fer the trail."

"Yeah, old man Sinclair busted his men an' Wild Bob's gang out this mornin'...They gave Gomer an' his fiancé a good workin' over...Why we're here. Need to deputize you to watch things while we're gone," said Flynn as they rode up to Lisanne's house and corrals together.

"I kin do that."

Slim glanced around and saw the filly in the round pen. "That's fair strange. Don't see Lisanne anywheres...Say, looky yonder." He pointed at the still form on the ground just outside the pen.

They trotted their horses over to the training ring.

"Oh, my Lord," said Fiona. "Who's that?"

"Jumpin' horny toads, it's Buster," exclaimed Slim as he jumped from his horse and ran to the inert figure.

The others also quickly dismounted and followed.

"Your new hired hand?" asked Flynn as they ran over to join Slim bending over the young man.

"Lisanne was breakin' 'im in on the horses when I left," answered Slim.

He yelled toward the barn and then the house. "Lisanne!...Lisanne!" Slim turned to Flynn. "Her horse ain't in its trap...She's gone."

"Look at all these tracks," said Fiona as she pointed at the fresh hoof prints around the pen.

"Uh, oh," commented Bone looking at Flynn. "This what I think it is?"

The sheriff grimaced. "'Fraid so...Hell an' damnation!" He stomped around in a tight circle.

"He still alive?" asked Loraine as she knelt beside Slim who was feeling of Buster's neck for a pulse.

"Yeah, jest barely...Gotta git 'im to town, quick though." He jerked his bandanna from around his neck and handed it to Loraine. "See as you can slow the bleedin' down whilst I go hitch up the buckboard."

Loraine ripped Buster's shirt back and pressed the kerchief against the hole in his side. Fiona brought a clean towel from a pannier on Potawatomi, the pack horse, for the larger exit wound in his back.

Bone looked around Buster's form. "Boy lost a lot of blood." He glanced off to the left toward the barn. "Shot him from over there while he was goin' over the fence…"

"Probably tryin' to get that shotgun," added Flynn pointing at the 12 gauge still leaning against the pen.

Fiona had gotten up, letting Loraine minister to Buster's wounds and examined the hoof prints. "Not enough tracks. I only see Sinclair and his men…Wild Bob's gang isn't with them."

"Figured they'd split up. Just did it sooner than I expected," said Flynn.

"Now what?" asked Bone.

Mason glanced over at the big man. "We split up, too." He paused a moment in thought. "Since neither of you track…Bone, you'll go with Fiona after the Sinclair bunch." Flynn looked at his partner. "You come with me, Loraine...you don't mind?"

"Whoa up there," Slim said to the sorrel gelding as the buckboard pulled up next to Loraine and Buster.

He had piled a number of empty tow sacks in the bed of the wagon to pad the hard wood flooring.

"Big man, you an' the sheriff help load 'im in the back here," he said as he unchained the tailgate.

"Can do," replied Bone.

They carefully lifted the unconscious teenager as Slim jumped up in the back to help position him on the sacks.

"Know you got to hurry, Slim, but take it easy as you can. He's pretty weak," said Loraine. "I got the bleeding mostly stopped, at least for now."

"Yessum," he replied as he climbed in the spring-loaded bench seat and unwrapped the reins from the brake lever.

"Come up there, Ted," Slim said as he flicked the ribbons over the horse's rump.

Flynn and the others watched the buckboard roll down the road toward the entrance.

"Think the boy will be all right?" asked Bone.

Ken Farmer

"If that rough-assed road into town don't kill 'im," said Flynn.

"I suspect Slim'll take it easy as he can," replied Fiona.

"Yeah...Well, folks, we got some backtrackin' to find out where they split up...Best take care of any business you need to now...Got some hard ridin' to do," said Flynn. "Since there's only four in the gang an' Bob's gun hand is shot up, shouldn't take us too long...We'll join ya'll soon as we can."

"There'll be some weeping and gnashing of teeth before this is over...and it won't be by us," said Fiona as her steel-gray eyes flashed with determination.

BOX CANYON

Sinclair, his men, and Lisanne pulled rein at the outer edge of the canyon.

"Let me go in alone. He an' his mares will spook if ya'll go in with me."

"Carter, you follow her in, but stay out of sight of the horses."

"Right, Pa," said the youngest as he dismounted and handed his reins to his brother, Rowdy.

He nodded at Lisanne. "Lead on, girl."

She looked daggers at him, turned and worked her way through the scrub oak, mesquite, and cedar trees toward the opening in the center of the canyon where a spring flowed from the hillside and created a small clear pool.

Lisanne began humming the nearer she got to the edge of the clearing. As she walked slowly out of the brush, Steeldust threw up his head, nickered and pawed the ground with a front foot.

She moved easily up to him as he stood a little ways from his herd watching over them.

Lisanne talked soothingly to the stallion as she petted him and slipped a braided horsehair halter over his head. She continued her humming.

She led him back out to Sinclair and the others by the attached ten foot *mekate* after motioning to Carter to stay back.

"Best let me lead him. Don't think he'll tolerate anyone else...'specially your men. He'll remember them from before," she said to Sinclair.

"Don't care, long as he don't slow us down. Just remember, he gets loose and we won't need you any longer…Understand me?"

Lisanne pursed her lips tightly and nodded.

JACK COUNTY

Fiona led the group of law officers back along the trail to the Flying L.

"Well, look here, they angled off to the box canyon where Lisanne left Steeldust and his herd…Makes sense. Sinclair wants that stallion."

She scouted around the entrance to the canyon. "Here's where they came out…Lisanne is leading an unshod horse…"

"Steeldust," interjected Flynn.

They followed the tracks on back to the original trail. She bumped Spot to a halt and glanced to the south.

"Here's where Wild Bob and his gang split off. I'd say they're headed toward the Brazos," she said. "Looks like this is where we separate, too."

"Yep. Ready Loraine?" asked Flynn.

"Always. I'll follow you," she replied.

Flynn dismounted and unpacked some of the supplies from Potawatomi's panniers and distributed them in his and Loraine's saddlebags. He swung back into Laddie's saddle.

"Newton, you go with mama," said Flynn as he pointed.

The border collie trotted over to Fiona and Bone.

"Ya'll watch your backs."

Flynn nodded. "Ain't new to this game, Bone. This is my kind of chase."

Fiona turned to the big man. "Bone, I'll track, you keep an eye peeled for ambush sites to the front and sides…I'm counting on you. Newton will let us know of anything that isn't as it should be. He and Spot have great instincts. "

"That's a good thing…I know you don't know what it is, but I was a Recon Marine over in Afghanistan. Kinda like guerrilla fightin'…and in similar terrain. With this .45-70, if I can see it, I can hit it."

"He can, too," added Loraine.

"I thought the Marines were on ships," said Fiona.

"We are. The Navy takes us to where we need to go and we hit the ground. Most of our work is behind enemy lines…lot of it at night," said Bone.

"I figure both of these gangs are back shooters," said Flynn.

"Learned to keep my head on a swivel. Been shot at mor'n once."

"You're a big target. Ever been hit?" asked Fiona.

He grinned. "Not yet."

Flynn looked off to the northwest at the dark line just above the horizon. "Uh, oh, looks like a storm comin'. Goin' to have to hook 'em up an' at least confirm the line the two groups have taken in case there's a heavy rain in that cloud bank."

"My guess is we have about an hour an' a half or so," commented Bone.

"Enough time to find some kind of shelter…maybe," added Fiona. "I see some green in the wall." She turned to Bone. "Let's go, big man."

Fiona legged Spot to the west, following the Sinclair's tracks. Newton followed alongside.

"How many we tailin', Marshal?" Bone asked as they trotted across the hills of north central Texas.

STEELDUST

Fiona glanced back down at the ground. "I make it eight, not counting Lisanne and the stallion."

"Eight to two." He chuckled. "Bet they don't know how much trouble they're in."

"Uh, huh, I'd say it's pretty even." She glanced out of the corner of her eye at him.

"My kinda odds," said Bone.

They looked at the growing dark cloud bank barreling at them from their right.

"I think they're headed toward the *Llano Estacado*...going to cross into New Mexico."

"Yep, the Staked Plains. Me and my captain done a lot of quail huntin' in that area. Lots of arroyos, coolies an' gullies...Not as flat an' barren as a lot of folks think," said Bone.

"No, but we need to find a ridge or creek bottom to shelter in pretty quick."

"One thing about it, they'll have to shelter up too," said Bone as the first peal of thunder rumbled across the plains like distant artillery.

§§§

CHAPTER FIFTEEN

BRAZOS CANYON

Flynn and Loraine trotted their horses south along a little used ranch road until he held up his hand to halt at the tree line. There was a two hundred yard open area between the trees and a high ridge of jumbled rocks and outcrops up ahead.

"See that limestone thrust up yonder?"

"Uh, huh."

It's the edge of the Palo Pinto Mountains…prime place for an ambush," he said.

"Then the Brazos is on the other side?"

He glanced over at her. "In the middle…Been there?"

"In our time…Bone and I were on a fishing trip to Possum Kingdom."

"Possum Kingdom? What's that?"

"They damned up the Brazos River…Made one hell of a lake."

"I can believe that." Flynn pointed at the ridge. "The river cuts through those mountains…created a deep set of canyons, filled with caves an' thick wooded bottoms along the water way an' its tributaries."

"Most of it's underwater in our time…Bone and I took shelter in one of those caves above the water line during a strange storm with a weird fog. Had ancient Indian symbols carved around it…Next thing we knew…we got caught up in some kind of anomaly and were transported to this time."

"Wow, that just staggers the imagination."

"You're telling me."

"Well, those canyons an' caves made ideal hideouts for the Commanche back twenty years ago…along with outlaws on the scout still today."

"Is that why Wild Bob an' his gang headed here?"

"I'd say." He looked at the line of black clouds creeping ever closer and watched as the horizontal lightning skipped along the edge of the front from cloud to cloud followed fifteen seconds later by rolling thunder.

Flynn reached back in his saddlebags and pulled out his binoculars from his cavalry days. "Here, give that ridge a good scan an'…." He handed Loraine the glasses.

"I know, look for movement and reflections."

"My gut feelin' is they're already on the other side in the first shelter they could find."

A spurt of dirt and dust fifteen feet in front of them kicked up into the air, followed a half-second later by the echoing boom of a rifle."

"Oops, wrong again. Back up under those trees." He indicated the copse of post oaks and mesquite at the side of the rutted dirt road.

Loraine and Flynn drew their Winchesters from their scabbard as they got under the branches.

"You take three feet the right side of that white cloud of gunsmoke an' fire two shots…I'll do the same to the left an' then we'll both shoot in the middle…Aim high, that Yellowboy doesn't have the power my '86 does."

Six rounds sounded almost as one as Loraine and Flynn fired as rapidly as they could work the levers.

"Well, we might have gotten lucky," Loraine commented as she lowered the rifle from her shoulder.

"Or at least scared the pee out of the shooter…Sounded like he shot a Henry."

"That why he was short?"

"My guess. Either that or he's a damn poor shot."

They waited a few more moments as the wind carried the gunsmoke away.

"No return fire," said Mason.

Loraine zeroed the field glasses in. "I see him…Going over the top. It's the skinny one…He's limping."

"Musta got a piece of him," said Flynn. "Awright, tell you what do. We'll ride at a hard gallop across the open space in case there's anybody else up there…Be harder to hit."

Loraine glanced at him. "Easy for you to say, but I'm with you…Go."

They each spurred their mounts to a wide open run until they reached the rocks. There were no shots fired in their direction.

After reining up in the cover of the first edge of boulders, Flynn raised up in his stirrups to look over the top.

"Think they've gone to ground…Be a good idea for us too, 'fore that storm gets here."

"Got any place in mind?" asked Loraine.

"Yeah, 'bout half way to the top there's a shallow cave just big enough for us an' the horses."

"Cave?"

"Not sure I'd call it a cave…more like sort of a notch in the face of the rock just big enough."

"Told you that's how we got here…In a cave during a storm," said Loraine.

Flynn grinned. "Reckon we'll find out, Miss Rodriquez. Come on."

JACK COUNTY

"That a creek up there?" asked Bone, pointing.

Fiona nodded. "Squaw Mountain Creek. Should be enough cover down in the bottom…Let's go."

They nudged their mounts to a gallop toward the tree line with Newton running alongside. Reining up at the edge, they dismounted and walked the animals into the woods, following a game trail toward the creek.

The path led to the edge of a drop off with an old buffalo cut down the steep bank to the thirty-foot wide canopied waterway and up the other side.

"Let's snug up against the west side of the creek bank. It's almost vertical and there's a good cover of trees overhead," said Fiona as the first down draft hit the woods after they got to the bottom.

The treetops overhead bent to the force of the wind as the air suddenly took on a decided chill.

Multiple bolts of lightning crackled around the area creating continuous rolling thunder. They held tightly to the animal's headstalls and patted the sides of their necks to keep them calm.

Newton crawled underneath and between Spot's legs and crossed his paws over his nose.

"Works for me," replied Bone, pulling out the yellow slicker from behind his cantle Fiona and

Loraine got for him when they picked up supplies at Barber's Mercantile.

The horses and Fiona's mule laid their ears back and dropped their heads down to protect their eyes and keep water out of their ears as they endured the onslaught.

Pea-size hail started peppering the leaf canopy overhead, rapidly changing to walnut-size stones. The leaves and branches deflected most of the hail, but some made their way through, bouncing off Bone and Fiona's hats and their saddles.

"Ow, that one hurt," said the marshal as a large one ricocheted off her shoulder.

The hail changed to a driving rain, further bending the tree tops and dropping broken limbs and leaves all about the creek bottom.

"Damn, this is a dandy," commented Bone. "Listen…think I hear a tornado."

The roaring sound similar to a runaway train reached their ears.

"Sounds that way a couple hundred yards," Bone said as he pointed up the creek to the north.

"Let's hope it stays that way," Fiona replied.

"Damn, like bein' under a waterfall." Bone pulled the collar of his slicker up around his neck.

"Starting to slack off a bit."

"Yeah, but don't want to get cocky though."

"Why?" asked Fiona.

"Ain't over."

"'O, full of scorpions is my mind!' wrote Shakespeare in *Macbeth*."

"Huh?"

Fiona grinned. "You're just like Mason...Tell you later."

"Probably a good reason," Bone mumbled.

She looked up as glimpses of blue sky behind the front began to show through the branches overhead. "Do what?"

"Nothin'."

A mile and a half to the north, the Sinclair bunch with Lisanne and Steeldust took refuge from the storm in the same creek bottom.

The tornado roared between them and Fiona and Bone. It brushed the tops of the trees, rose back up into the clouds, and then back down to the ground on the east side of the creek, slinging branches and debris a hundred yards on each side.

"Good thing we found this creek," said Carter ducking a falling limb.

"We didn't find it, idiot, it's been here all the time," said his father.

"I was just thinkin'…"

"You don't have the brains to think…You leave that to me."

"Uh…right, Pa."

Lisanne kept Steeldust calm by humming to him and stroking the side of his muscular neck.

The sun was nearing the western horizon as the last of the storm moved its inexorable way east.

"I suggest we clear some of these branches and just pitch camp right here," said Fiona.

"Good for me…Betcha they're doin' the same," replied Bone.

"You mind taking the animals up top to some grass and hobble them while I get a fire started?"

"Can do."

"Let them drink first."

"Right."

The evening night sounds, crickets, birds and frogs, after the storm started their cacophony of music. Bone led the animals up the narrow buffalo trail to the top of the bank where there was some tender grasses and hobbled them.

STEELDUST

JACKSBORO, TEXAS

"Looks like my clinic is filling up," said Mosier.

"We only have one more bed," commented his nurse, Gertrude. "Now that the storm is past, I'll go down to Ruth Ann's and get some of her bone broth."

The doctor glanced over at Buster with concern on his face. "Bullet missed his liver by less than a half an inch before it exited out his back between his ribs or he wouldn't still be with us…Still, boy lost a lot of blood…Bone broth will be good when he wakes up from the ether."

"I'll get my sister to come sit this evenin' with them to give us both a break. You spent over four hours in surgery with that young man," she said.

Mosier nodded. "Good thing they're both young. Older men wouldn't have survived either the gunshot or the beating."

The small clinic smelled strongly of alcohol and ether from the recent surgery. Emma Lou sat beside Gomer's bed, holding his hand and looked questioningly up at the doctor.

He lifted one of the deputy's eyelids and took a look at his small pupil, pursed his lips and glanced back at the young girl. "No change, but his pulse and breathing are steady and that's a good thing...so far. His mind has withdrawn so his body can deal with the pain and the trauma."

§§§

CHAPTER SIXTEEN

BRAZOS RIVER BOTTOM

Flynn and Loraine stepped away from their cover under the overhanging ledge of limestone as the storm front pushed on east.

"Well, it was a hard enough rain, with that hail and wind, that I'm sure any tracks washed away," said Mason.

"Let's go check where the shooter was. If we hit him, there may be some sign left. Blood spatter is hard to wash away," replied Loraine.

"That some of your police work from your time?"

"Bone and I specialize in blood spatter and crime scene investigation."

"Interesting. I'll follow you this time."

They walked their horses out and in the direction of where they believed the ambusher had fired from.

Five minutes later, they tied their mounts to some post oak saplings and worked over to what appeared to be the most logical site, a refrigerator-sized boulder.

"Here we go," said Loraine as she picked up a casing. ".44?" She pitched it to Flynn.

".44-40 rimfire. Yep, a Henry."

"Ah, look at the side of this rock." Loraine pointed to several dark spots. "Blood."

"Think you're right."

"See the thick side with the thin side pointing this way?"

"Yeah...What does that mean?"

"Shows the direction the impact came from that caused the wound…Us."

"Oh, right, I see…Interesting," Flynn noted.

Loraine followed the blood trail staining some of the tall grasses and rocks up toward the ridge. "The rain washed the tracks and blood from the soil, but not from the grasses, leaves and rocks…See?"

"Yeah, there's a lot of it, too."

"Think one of us hit an artery…Most likely his femoral, considering the way he was limping," said Loraine.

They topped the crest and headed down the other side.

"I see a foot sticking out from the back of that jumble of rocks," observed Flynn.

They walked around a small boulder. Flynn rolled the body over with his foot.

"Dead…Got two holes in ''im, side and leg…I'd say he bled out."

"Excellent observation, Sheriff…Wonder who he was?"

"Got a dodger on him an' the rest of Wild Bob's gang couple weeks ago…Think this one is Caleb 'Stringbean' Barton. Five hunderd dollar reward on 'im."

"Well, one less to worry about," said Loraine.

"Yep." Flynn glanced west at the sun settling on the horizon. "Might as well find a place to pitch camp."

"I'm with you."

SQUAW MOUNTAIN CREEK

Fiona had built a hat-sized fire for their coffee and supper. She grabbed the pot with her folded over deerskin glove.

"More coffee?"

"Thought you'd never ask...By the way, the bacon and beans were good, but these pickled peaches are awesome...My grandma used to make 'em."

Bone stabbed a slice of one with his Benchmade folding knife and popped it in his mouth. "Mmm, good." He wiped the juice from his chin with the back of his hand.

She grinned. "Thank you, sir. *My* grandmother taught me how. She'd put a case of them by in the pantry during peach season...I like them better than canned sweet ones, except for cobbler…but even that's pretty good."

"Can't wait to try your cobbler…Oh, don't be upset if you wake up an' happen to notice I'm gone durin' the night."

"What do you mean?"

"Remember, I told you I was a Recon Marine over in Afghanistan?"

"Uh, huh."

"It was called Black Ops."

"Black Ops?"

"Secret operations…I'm also an *at-large* member of an ultra Black Ops unit know as the Black Eagle Force."

"And that is?"

"It's above top secret…Our motto is: You didn't see us…This didn't happen…We don't exist…We are the Black Eagle Force."

"That's amazing."

"Well, our specialty is behind the lines night work…You'll notice I avoid looking at the fire."

"I did. It ruins your ability to see in the darkness, doesn't it?"

"Right...Newton an' I are going to go find Lisanne...Don't think they'll be expecting visitors tonight."

The red and white Border Collie woofed and spun around twice.

"How?"

Bone grinned. "It's what I do...You be okay while I'm gone?"

It was her turn to grin. "Oh, I think so. Been tracking outlaws on the scout for a number of years, now. Besides, my mule, Spot, is as good a watchdog as Newton."

The dog cocked his head at her.

"He's a *watchmule*, then?" suggested Bone with a big grin.

"You could say that...Does *okay* mean all right?"

"Yeah, we use it all the time."

"Must have come from the Choctaw word, *okeh*, which is used as an affirmative reply to a question."

"Think I said that."

"Too bad you don't have some moccasins like the ones I carry in my saddlebags for quiet work...big as you are."

"That would be nice, but we're trained to move pretty quietly when we work behind enemy lines…especially going inside their camps."

"Like an Apache or a Seminole."

"Pretty close…'Course I've got a major advantage didn't have overseas."

"That would be?"

Bone held up his right wrist. "The bracelet Lucy gave me in my time."

"Oh, right. It…"

"Bends light around the wearer for about three feet…"

"Similar to Persus' cap of invisibility, then…He was Hercules' great-grandfather."

Bone shook his head as he got to his feet. "If you say so." He pulled a bone-handled, ten inch Bowie from the sheath on his web belt, tested the edge, and then put it back. "Thanks for pickin' up this knife for me at the mercantile. Almost good as a K-Bar."

"That's a knife, also, I take it."

Bone nodded. "Uh, huh. Best combat knife in the world. Official knife of the Marine Corps."

He looked at Newton, then up at the mottled light filtering through the canopy overhead from the gibbous moon well above the horizon. "Might as well go now, son…dark enough an' the shadows help." He turned and started north along the creek bank.

"You're going to stay down here in the bottom?"

"I suspect they took shelter down here like we did…and pitched camp down here, like we did."

"You sound like Bass Reeves…Don't follow them, go where they're going to be."

"That's right, you worked with the legendary Bass Reeves, didn't you?"

"How did you know that?"

He smiled over his shoulder. "It's a gift," Bone said as he and Newton disappeared into the darkness.

Carter Sinclair walked out of the flickering light from the campfire next to the creek. He nodded to Baker. "Got this. Go get yourself a cup of coffee, Cullen…Take your time comin' back."

The gunhawk grinned, nodded knowingly and headed toward the fire.

"Well, looks like it's just me an' you this time, Missy," he said with a sardonic smile.

STEELDUST

Lisanne struggled against her bonds. Her hands were tied behind her back and her feet were bound together.

Carter pulled out his belt knife, reached down and sliced the cotton clothesline rope around her ankles. He forced a knee between her legs and ripped her chambray shirt apart exposing her small tight breasts.

"You better kill me when you're done, you piece of crap, because I'm surely goin' to kill you…Don't know when or where, but somehow…I will kill you," she hissed.

"Umm, I like feisty." He rose up on both knees and started unbuttoning his jeans…

BRAZOS CANYON

Flynn had dug a small fire pit surrounded by large boulders. They were having their after dinner coffee.

"You make as good a pot of coffee as my Fiona does, Loraine."

"Thank you, kind sir. I'm usually tasked as the official coffee maker in the station."

183

"What's a station?"

"It's what we call the police office. We have some fifteen patrol officers and six detectives or investigators…Not counting our captain and two lieutenants…I make a lot of coffee, if Bone and I aren't on a case outside."

"What type of cases do ya'll mostly work on?"

"Usually murder, but sometimes other things like physical harassment…It's how Bone met Lucy."

"Oh?"

"Some oil company wanted her land and threatened to burn her out. She was expecting to be rescued anytime and it was Bone who stepped in took care of the situation…It's why she gave him and his Padrino her ranch and that bracelet when she left."

"So she finally got rescued?"

"Uh, huh…In 2014."

A pack of coyotes began tuning up and singing their night song down the draw a few hundred yards.

"Ohh, that gives me the creeps," said Loraine.

"Not been out campin' in the wild much, I take it."

"No...The fishing trip we were on when we stumbled into the Indian portal that brought us here was the first time...Look. What's that?" She pointed several hundred yards across the other side of the creek at a barely visible glow reflecting against a large boulder.

"Well, well, believe they weren't as careful with their campfire as we are."

§§§

CHAPTER SEVENTEEN

SQUAW MOUNTAIN CREEK

A thick muscular arm encircled Carter's throat, lifted him off Lisanne, and tightened against both sides, shutting off not only his breath, but also the blood supply to his brain. "You're goin' to think feisty, you little jerk," whispered Bone directly into his ear.

STEELDUST

He held the pressure on the young Sinclair's neck as the boy briefly clawed at the steel banded arm and kicked his feet ineffectually in the air. Carter's eyes bugged out as a silent scream formed in his mouth.

In twenty more seconds, his body went limp as a dishrag. Vertebrae cracked audibly as Bone gave him one last extra squeeze by flexing his biceps and dropped his body to the side like a pile of dirty laundry.

"Shhh." He placed a finger on Lisanne's lips as Newton crawled up on his belly and licked the side of her face. "Roll over."

She nodded and turned over to her side so he could cut the rope around her wrists.

Bone stood up and touched two of the turquoise colored crystals on his solid gold bracelet. The air around him shimmered as he stepped back away from her into a dark shadow.

"Hey, baby brother, save me some of the good stuff," said his older brother, Al, from a few feet away in the shadows. "Come get me when…"

He never finished as Bone clapped a thick hand over his mouth from behind, slipped the Bowie between his ribs, into his heart—and twisted. It wasn't necessary.

Bone quietly lowered the dead man to the ground and touched the stones again. The air shimmered once more and he became visible in the mottled shadows.

He eased back to Lisanne who was squatting down with her arm around Newton, her eyes big as saucers. She had pulled her shirt back over her breasts, buttoned the one button that was left and tucked it into her canvas trousers.

Bone picked her up. She wrapped her arms around his neck and nestled her head against his broad chest as he carried her back to the south as quietly as he and Newton had come.

A hundred yards back down the creek, he set her on her feet.

"You all right?"

"Am now…How did you find me and how the heck did you do that disappearin' thing back there?" she asked sotto voce.

Bone grinned and started back off toward his and Fiona's camp. "Magic."

"Uh, huh…Let me have your knife."

He stopped and turned. "Thinkin' about goin' back and killin' somebody?"

"No. Gotta cut Steeldust free. The horses are hobbled up on top above the creek on some graze."

"We can't take him with us."

"Don't intend to...Just gonna cut him loose. He'll find his herd on his own," Lisanne said.

"Right." He unsheathed the Bowie again, flipped it over in the air, and handed it to her, handle first.

Twenty minutes later, they stole into camp.

"Got any coffee left," Bone's deep bass voice said from the shadows.

Startled, Fiona jumped to her feet, both Colts instantly in her hands pointing at Bone and Lisanne as they walked into the flickering firelight.

"My God, Bone, neither Spot nor I heard ya'll coming...Like to have scared me to death, not counting almost shooting you."

He laughed. "Told you that's what I do...Look who I got."

Fiona slipped her Peacemakers back in their holsters and rushed over to hug Lisanne.

"Oh, Fiona, thank ya'll so much." She glanced over at Bone as he sat down on a log. "He was just in time...They killed Buster."

She released the teenager. "Maybe not, honey. He was still alive when we got there. Slim took him into town to Doctor Mosier."

She sunk to her knees. "Oh, thank God…They also killed his family, includin' his baby sister…The 'animals' burned her alive in their house."

"Oh, my sweet Jesus. How?" asked Fiona.

"She was in her crib when they set fire to the Martin's house…Buster said they rode off laughin'."

Bone got back to his feet, the muscles in his jaw rippling. "Worthless bastards will get no quarter from me…They'll die where they stand."

Fiona glanced at the big man and nodded, her lips tightly pursed. "Going to have to temporarily forget we're law officers."

"Got that right," concurred Bone.

Then Fiona turned back to Lisanne. "You all right? Hungry? Or need coffee?"

"Would take some coffee," Lisanne said as she got back to her feet.

Fiona picked up two cups, filled them from the pot and handed them to Bone and Lisanne. "So, tell me."

Bone squatted down, blew across the top of the cup, took a sip, and then looked back up at Fiona. "Well, let's just say we only have six bad guys to worry about now."

"No one heard you?"

Bone looked up with a wry grin.

She nodded. "Right."

"They also don't have any horses," added Lisanne after having a sip of her own coffee.

Bone glanced in surprise at her.

"How so?" asked Fiona.

"I borrowed Bone's knife to cut Steeldust's hobbles an' free him." She smiled big. "Decided to cut their horses loose while I was at it...They followed him when he headed back toward his mares."

"Good move, girl," said Bone as he leaned over and held up his huge hand.

Lisanne looked at it with a puzzled expression.

"Slap it," said Bone.

She reached up and slapped the monstrous palm with a resounding thwack.

"We call that a 'high-five' back home...It means congratulations or good job."

"I like it," Lisanne replied as she held her hand up for Fiona.

"I like it, too," the marshal said as she slapped it. "At least we know where the rest of them will be tomorrow."

They looked up as a big yellow lab padded down the creek bank, slinking low and wagging his bushy tail as he approached his mistress.

"Barney! You found me." Lisanne wrapped her arms around his neck and gave him a hug.

Newton approached, wagging his tail, also, at the appearance of his friend.

They exchanged smells and promptly laid down together beside Lisanne.

"It's nice to have friends," she said.

BRAZOS CANYON

"Well, shall we?" asked Flynn.

"Like Bone always says in situations like this...Might as well do it...Can't dance," replied Loraine.

"He's an unusual fellow."

"You don't know the half of it...Wait till he puts hot pepper sauce in your coffee or beer."

"He would do that?"

Loraine raised her eyebrows.

"Oh, yeah," Flynn said. "Think we should build up our fire so they'll know we're here."

"And slip over there while they're keeping an eye on it."

"Right you are."

Flynn started putting more logs and sticks on their small fire. Soon it was blazing high.

"They should be able to see that," commented Loraine.

"I'd say...Goin' to take your rifle?"

"Don't believe so. I'll use my Kimber. May need to crank out a few rounds quickly. We call it CQC."

"CQC?"

"Close Quarter Combat...self explanatory."

"See your point. I'll bring my sawed off 10 gauge coach gun."

Loraine nodded. "That'll work...Lead out, sir."

Thirty minutes later, they had worked down their side of the draw, across the narrow feeder creek to the Brazos and up the other side.

Ken Farmer

"You take this side. Give me five minutes to circle around to the other…then you step out between those two boulders," said Flynn. "If they try to make a fight of it…"

"I'll take that tall drink of water first, you get the stocky one…We can save Wild Bob to the last since he has that useless right hand."

"Good thinkin'," Flynn whispered as he turned and faded into the shadows.

"Looks like they're camped over yonder," said Garth, the tall outlaw as he pointed out the fire flickering across the creek.

"Keep an eye on it. We'll slip up in the rocks before dawn right after that moon sets…be dark enough." Bob held out his cup with his good hand for Bo, the stocky man, to fill. "Then when they come over lookin' for us, we'll ambush 'em, an' then disappear into the canyons."

"They musta got Stringbean, er he'd a been back by now," said Bo as he set the pot back down on a flat rock beside the fire.

"Yeah, coulda used that rifle. Sinclair's a sorry bastard, only givin' us one," said Garth.

194

"Did bust us out, though," commented Bob. "Gotta give 'im that."

"These handguns'll be enough to take care of them lawdogs when we surprise 'em," said Bo as he drew his and twirled it about his finger like the gunhawk he thought he was.

"Speakin' of surprise...hands up, boys," said Flynn as he stepped out of the shadows with the scattergun held at his hip.

"Son of a bitch!" exclaimed Bo as he swung around to the voice, thumbing back the hammer on his .45.

Flynn squeezed both triggers on the Greener, blowing Bo backward five feet—the 24 double ought buckshot took most of his face and chest. The 10 gauge made a tremendous roar and created a huge cloud of gunsmoke.

"Hey!" came a shout from behind Garth as he drew his Colt and turned toward the sheriff. He spun completely back around, aimed at Loraine as his finger started to squeeze his trigger.

He was never able to finish the action as Loraine, in a modified Weaver stance with both hands on her .45, double tapped him in the chest—the holes less than two millimeters apart. She placed a third round between his eyes. The three shots sounded as almost as one from her Kimber semiautomatic.

Wild Bob took advantage of the large white cloud from the shotgun blast to drop to the ground. The right-handed man grabbed for his pistol with his left, fumbling a little as he did so. He recovered, laid his gun across his right wrist, aimed in Flynn's direction, and fired.

The shot plucked at the sheriff's shirt sleeve and plowed a shallow furrow across his biceps.

Bob only got the one shot off as two rounds from Loraine penetrated the back of his head. A fine mist of blood along with pieces of his skull and brain matter sprayed out in front of him, some of it landing in the fire where it popped and sizzled on the burning logs.

Flynn stepped forward, glanced at Bob, and then looked closely at Garth's body across the fire. "Jesus, Mary and Joseph, Loraine, can't lay my finger between the two holes in his chest…Gotta get me one of those semiautomatics."

She grinned. "Afraid you'll have to wait about another twelve years. The first one like mine will be a Colt 1911A."

"I only heard two shots." He pointed to Garth and back over to Wild Bob. "How many did you fire?"

Loraine shrugged her shapely shoulders. "Five." Flynn shook his head. "My, God."

He looked around again. "We'll just have to leave 'em for the critters...Take their weapons. Need to catch up with Fiona an' Bone...They got eight to two odds."

Loraine smiled big. "Sounds about even to me...You don't know Bone."

§§§

CHAPTER EIGHTEEN

SQUAW MOUNTAIN CREEK

Algernon Sinclair sat on a log near the fire, holding his head in both hands, his body shook with silent sobs. The bodies of his oldest and youngest sons lay at his feet.

He finally lifted his head and glanced around at his middle son, Rowdy, and three of the remaining four gunhawks.

"You sorry sons of bitches let them lawdogs just waltz in here, kill my two boys and make off with the split-tail…Damn you…damn you to hell." He paused and stared at the ground.

"Sorry, Pa." Rowdy looked at the others. "We just…"

"Shut up! Just shut the hell up…There's nothing you can say to bring your brothers back."

"What are we goin' to do now, Mister Sinclair?" asked Baker.

"We're goin' after 'em. They're going to pay and…"

Fats McClure stumbled down the steep bank from the top. "Mister Sinclair! Mister Sinclair…They're gone!"

The patriarch got to his feet. "Who's gone?"

"The horses! All the horses is gone. Somebody cut their hobbles…Even the pack horse." He held the hobbles up in his right hand. "They're all gone…We're shanks mare."

"Son of a green bitch!" Sinclair stomped around in a tight circle twice, stopped and pointed a finger at Cullen Baker. "It's your fault…You were on guard."

Baker shook his head. "I know, Mister Sinclair, an' I'm sorry as I can be…but Carter come out an' told me to git a cup of coffee. Said he wanted to try some of that gal an'…"

"I don't want to hear it. Dammit to hell…I don't want to hear it. My boys gone…They're gone…How the hell did they kill Carter. There's not a mark on him."

"Uh, his neck was broke, Mister Sinclair," said Frenchy.

"Damnation…Must have been that big bastard ya'll told me about…Don't understand how he didn't make any noise. Him and the woman marshal, both, must have come right in our camp."

He stopped, took a deep breath and put his hands on his hips. "They gotta be reasonably close. Scatter out. Find 'em and report back to me…Got that?"

"Want us to go now, Pa? Or wait till the mornin'?" asked Rowdy.

"No! Next week, you ignorant…Why am I surrounded by such idiots…Go! Go. Get out of my sight and find 'em…Now!"

A mile and a half from the Sinclair camp, Bone, Fiona and Lisanne were making dummy bedrolls just at the edge of the light cast by the fire.

"Don't think there's any question they're gonna come lookin'...In case they come down this far..."

Fiona interrupted Bone. "They'll see the bedrolls in the shadows and think it's us...And we'll be on both sides of the creek bank above the camp."

"Right, Marshal. Now, could be they'll spread out lookin' for us or could be they'll be lookin' as a group...So first thing, let's move the stock down the creek aways further from the Sinclair camp than we are here...Lisanne, that's your job." He handed her his Peacemaker. "In case they happen to come upon you."

"What are you goin' to use?" she asked.

Bone patted the big S&W .50 cal on his hip.

She grinned and nodded.

"You can use a handgun, can't you, honey?" asked Fiona.

"I'm better with a rifle, but I can hit what I aim at."

"Chances are you won't have to, but better to be safe," added Bone. "Now, let's build up the fire a bit an' see if we can draw them in...The moon'll be down soon…couple of hours or so before dawn…Be darker than three feet up a bull's butt."

Lisanne giggled at Bone's metaphor.

"We've got time, I believe, for another cup of coffee, before we do our thing," said Fiona.

"Expect so. They won't have any idea which direction we are from their camp. It'll take 'em a while to find us…Got an idea, too."

"What's that? asked Fiona.

"Oh, just a booby trap we learned from the Vietnamese in my time. Gonna put one or so up the creek bottom in case they come that way."

"What's a booby trap?" asked Lisanne.

"Well, it's a device to make the bad guys wonder what else is out there…It's called upsetting their homeostasis," said Bone.

"Their what?" she asked.

"Their feeling of well being," replied Fiona.

"Oh, got it…Make 'em nervous."

"Close enough," added Bone. "Now how 'bout that coffee?"

The gibbous moon disappeared below the western horizon. The millions upon millions of stars shown even more brightly in the black velvet of the sky after it went down.

Up on top of the creek bank, among their horses and Spot, Lisanne sat cross-legged, Indian style, in the blue stem and buffalo grass after she had moved them. Both Newton and Barney were at her side. She focused on the brightest star in the sky–Venus.

"'Star light, star bright, The first star I see tonight; I wish I may, I wish I might, Have the wish I wish tonight'."

The magnificent steeldust stallion stepped softly up to Lisanne, not disturbing her reverie, and stood towering above her for a moment. Then he leaned down and nuzzled her long blond hair and the side of her face and nickered softly.

Lisanne exhibited no surprise as she reached back and stroked his velvet muzzle. She turned her head and kissed his nose, "I love you, too, Steeldust."

Then she looked back up at the sky. "Thank you, sweet Jesus. Praise your holy name." Tears began to roll down her cheeks. "Thank you," she whispered with a lump in her throat and please help Buster, if you will.

She got to her feet, wrapped her arms around his muscular neck and pressed her face into his thick dark mane.

Two hundred yards up the creek from Bone and Fiona's camp, Frenchy carefully made his way along the bank down in the draw in the near pitch black darkness. He could make out an occasional flicker of a campfire through the intermittent brush and willows downstream.

He began to move faster with more confidence as he got closer and could make out the campfire including the three still forms around it.

Frenchy didn't see or feel the thin cotton fishing line trigger stretched low across the game trail until a three-inch thick black locust limb wrapped with thorny whoa vines was released and slapped him across the face. The impact of the whipsawing branch was enough to knock the big man to his back.

Both his hands went to his face, now bleeding from the numerous vicious thorns that raked across it and his chest, many of them embedded deeply in his skin, including one eye.

He rolled over to his knees moaning. "Ah, ah, ah...Oh, God, oh, God," he screamed as he staggered to his feet and then fell to his knees again.

Frenchy stumbled his way back up the creek toward the Sinclair camp, occasionally falling in the water.

"Bingo," mumbled a grinning Bone from halfway up the bank closer to their camp as he listened to the big man moan and stagger back up along the creek bed. "That's one more."

He worked his way back down to the camp. "Come on out, guys...They won't be back tonight. Just as well get some sleep."

Fiona and Lisanne came down the bank also, stepping into camp.

"Sounds good to me," Fiona agreed. "What type branch did you use?"

"Black locust. It has long, evil black thorns...Eat a man up."

"Uh, huh, familiar with it. The Indians use the long thorns as needles to sew leather with...Unbelievably sharp."

Bone sucked the blood dripping from a finger. "Tell me about it."

Rowdy, Fats and Cullen Baker made their way back into the camp.

"Well?" demanded Sinclair.

"Couldn't see our own feet after the moon went down, Pa...I didn't find nothin." He looked at the others.

Fats and Baker both shook their heads.

"Where's Frenchy?"

"He went down the creek, figured he'd a been back by now, too."

They all turned at the sounds of something crashing through the brush near the water to see the big man stagger into camp. He was covered in blood.

"Good God, man, what happened to you?" asked Sinclair as he nodded at the others to catch him before he fell into the fire.

Fats and Baker helped him to sit down in front of Sinclair.

"They're camped a mile or so downstream...set a trap 'long the trail," mumbled Frenchy.

"By the Lord Harry, looks like he's been drug behind a horse through the prickly pear," said Baker.

"Pull 'em out...Pull 'em out," Frenchy begged as he looked up at Fats with his one good eye that was beginning to swell shut.

"Git my fencin' pliers outta my saddlebags, Cullen. See as I kin do somethin' for this pore soul," said Fats. "Gotta hurt like hell."

"Got a better idea," said Sinclair as he drew his pistol and shot Frenchy in the forhead.

"What'd you do that for, Pa?" asked Rowdy.

"Don't have time to care for him...slow us down."

The morning sun was casting a pink glow into the gray sky above the eastern horizon. The songs of the blue jay and mocking bird were welcoming the new day.

"Get up, get up, you worthless scum. You got enough light now...go find those lawdogs, before the sun gets up," shouted Sinclair. "We got what we needed out of Frenchy...Now go."

"Me an' Cullen'll take the west side of the creek Fats, you go down the east," said Rowdy as they got about a hundred yards downstream. "When we get to their camp...just open fire. Kill the murderin' sons of bitches…kill 'em all right where they sleep. When you hear us start shootin', you open up, too, Fats. Got it?…An' watch out fer snares an' traps from them sneaky bastards like Frenchy run into."

The outlaws crept up to Bone and Fiona's camp. There was a thick layer of ground fog that settled down in the creek bottom as a result of yesterday's rain.

They could just make out the glow of the coals from the dying campfire and the three blanket covered forms surrounding it.

Rowdy nudged Cullen and each racked a shell in their Winchesters. They opened fire as fast as they could work the levers. Fats followed suit from thirty feet away on the other side of the creek.

The three men emptied their rifles at the three bedrolls before they stopped, ending the continuous roar.

"Well, nobody could live through that," said Rowdy as the thick cloud of gunsmoke from the forty-six rounds fired from the three rifles blended into the gray morning fog. "Let's go check it out…then find the horses."

STEELDUST

They stepped out of the bushes and into the campsite.

Rowdy laughed. "Got you, you big son of a..." He kicked the large form under the first blanket he came to...

§§§

CHAPTER NINETEEN

JACK COUNTY, TEXAS

"How far do you think they got?" asked Loraine as they easy-cantered their horses west while the sun was rising at their backs.

"Considerin' the storm, not too awful far, I'd think…Maybe as far as Squaw Mountain."

"Where is that?"

"'Almost fifteen miles further west of where we are now. They may have taken cover in the creek that runs along side it. It's in a deep draw that's canopied over by big pecan, hickory an' cottonwood trees...I've sheltered there myself a time or two." He pointed ahead in the direction they were traveling. "Looky yonder."

She peered toward the shadow in the still dark western horizon. "That flat topped hill in the distance?"

"Right...Squaw Mountain."

"That's a mountain?"

"Comparatively speakin'."

"Take your word for it," Loraine replied.

"We should be there in a 'bout an hour an' a half at this pace."

JACKSBORO, TEXAS

"I'm thirsty," said a groggy Buster Martin as he blinked his eyes and squinted over at a dozing Doctor Mosier sitting in a straight-backed chair.

The early morning sun was streaming through the window as the doctor snapped awake in an

211

instant and jumped to his feet. "Well, young man, glad to see you finally woke up."

"Where am I?" He glanced around the semi-dark room.

"Gertrude," he yelled.

In a few seconds, the nurse entered from the front office. "Yes, sir...Oh, my he's awake."

"Awake and thirsty," said the doctor.

"Be right back," she replied with a smile.

In a short moment, she came back in the clinic patient room with a thick glass tumbler two-thirds filled with water.

Gertrude leaned over Buster, lifted his head slightly and held the glass to his lips. After several swallows, he nodded.

"That was good, thank you...What happened?"

"You've been shot," answered Mosier.

"Oh...yeah. Seen the same men what killed my family ride around the corner of the barn an' I went for the shotgun." He looked back up at the doctor. "Guess I didn't make it."

Mosier raised his eyebrows. "Apparently not."

He felt of the bandages around his ribcage. "How's come I ain't dead?"

"You're a very lucky young man, Buster. Bullet went around the inside of your ribs and out the back. Didn't hit any vital organs or break any ribs...You bled quite a bit, though."

"That why I'm so weak?"

"It is." The doctor glanced over at his nurse. "Would you run down to Ruth Ann's and get Buster some broth?"

The matronly nurse looked at him over the top of her wire-rimmed glasses. "No, but I'll walk." She smiled as she started for the door.

"Can I have some too," came a voice from the next bed. "An' maybe somethin' for this headache I got."

"Gomer," exclaimed Emma Lou. "You're awake." She sat up in her bed.

He looked at her through his black swollen eyes. "Well, yeah. Sounded like a family reunion in here...Who can sleep with all this racket?" He tried to roll over to his side. "Oh, whizbang muffleshaw...I hurt all over more'n anywhere else."

Mosier chuckled and glanced back to his nurse. "Looks like it's going to be a good day after all, Gertrude. Think you're going to have to bring a tray...Wouldn't mind having some coffee, myself."

"Pot's on the stove in the front, you old goat, get it yourself. I've got work to do." She winked at him and headed out the door.

SQUAW MOUNTAIN CREEK

"Ow, ow, ow." Rowdy danced around on one foot, and then limped in a circle. "Dangomighty."

"What's the matter, Rowdy?" Baker asked as he poked one of the other bullet riddled blankets. "Oh, we been tricked."

"It was a damned log…Think I broke my foot," said Rowdy.

"That's not all boys," said Bone from up the bank a little ways. "This just ain't gonna be your day."

Bone squeezed the trigger on his big 500. The cannon-like explosion sent a 500 grain slug at 1500 feet per second completely through Rowdy's chest, exploding his heart. The massive round blew him to his back, dead when he hit the ground.

Fats and Baker both turned, panic firing indiscriminately into the trees up both sides of the creek with their .45s.

STEELDUST

Fiona sent two rounds from one of her .38-40 Peacemakers into Fats, spinning him around and into the creek.

She and Bone simultaneously shot Cullen Baker. Two rounds from Fiona slammed into his chest and one from Bone into his head, exploding it like a ripe melon.

JACK COUNTY, TEXAS

"Gunfire," exclaimed Flynn. "Comin' from near the mountain."

"That was Bone's .50 cal," said Loraine at the obviously louder sound mixed in with the others. "There it is again...It's a fire fight."

"Let's ride," Flynn shouted as he bumped his blue roan gelding, Laddie, in the ribs.

Loraine was right behind him.

SQUAW MOUNTAIN CREEK

The gunsmoke from Fiona and the Sinclair gang's guns slowly drifted up into the rising morning fog.

Bone and Fiona made their way down the creek bank, with their pistols at the ready.

"Don't believe there's any survivors," commented Bone.

"Yeah, but the patriarch of the clan, Algernon Sinclair, III, wasn't with them." She looked over at Bone. "He's still out there somewhere."

"Guess I better go find him then."

"Won't be hard," came a voice from behind some cedars downstream.

Fiona and Bone stopped and looked across the campsite to see Sinclair step out. He was holding Lisanne in front of him, his arm around her throat.

"I knew they would screw this up...I would suggest you put down those guns or I'll blow this little girl's head off." He put the muzzle of his .45 against the side of her head and thumbed back the hammer.

"You do and you won't live three seconds," said Bone as he and Fiona dropped their weapons.

"Don't give a damn. You two have killed all I had in this world...my boys. So I don't care if I live or die, but you're going to join me in hell."

"Maybe, maybe not," came another voice from up the bank.

Flynn and Loraine stepped out, their guns leveled in Sinclair's direction.

"Looks like a standoff," said Loraine. She looked over at Flynn. "You know, big as he is, I think I can hit a vital spot sticking out from behind Lisanne…Like his head."

"Don't worry, honey, she can shoot a fly off a bull's butt at thirty yards," commented Bone.

"The hell you say," shouted Sinclair.

A squeal sounded from behind him as Steeldust charged down the bank, sliding to a stop behind him in the sand and taking a plug out of Sinclair's left shoulder.

Lisanne took advantage of Steeldust's rescue, spun out of Sinclair's arm and dove back into the cedar trees.

"Damn you," Sinclair exclaimed as he aimed his Colt at the nearest law officer to him—Fiona.

"No!" screamed Bone, standing four feet beside and a little behind her as he launched his 6'8" frame in front of her, knocking her a step backward as Sinclair squeezed the trigger.

Bone took the round in his chest with the audible flat thump sound of a bullet striking flesh and crumpled to the ground.

Simultaneously, six rounds blasted Sinclair. He jerked like he had the Saint Vidus Dance.

The first two shots were from Fiona's left hand Colt, one tenth of a second later, two from Flynn, and three tenths of a second after that, two more from Loraine. All six holes in his chest could fit inside a saucer and in less than a half second.

"Bone! Bone!" Loraine screamed as she rushed to the big man's side and dropped to her knees in the sand.

He looked up at Fiona and then at Loraine. "Hey, Pard, glad you could make it." He coughed and blood and bubbles came out of the hole in his chest. "Don't hurt near as much as I thought it would...Ah," he moaned. "Spoke too soon." He coughed again, spitting up frothy blood.

Fiona knelt down beside him, jerked out a clean white handkerchief from her coat pocket and pressed it against the wound to staunch the flow of blood. She felt underneath him. "Didn't go through, but it clipped his lung...You saved my life, Bone."

"Had to...He was goin' to shoot you." More blood bubbled from his mouth.

Lisanne also knelt beside him. "How can I help?" she said as tears rolled down her cheeks.

"We've got to get him to a doctor," exclaimed Loraine as her eyes also filled with tears. "Damn you, Bone! Don't you die on me…Don't you die on me. You hear me?" she screamed in his face.

He looked up at her and whispered, "Don't have to yell, Pard, ain't on my list…Today."

His eyes closed as he slipped into unconsciousness.

"He's going into shock. Get some blankets. Elevate his feet," commanded Loraine.

"Lucy! We need Lucy," said Fiona.

"But, she's over thirty five miles away," commented Flynn.

Lisanne jumped up. "I'll get her. Just tell me exactly where she is."

Flynn looked at her. "I can tell you, but how…"

"Steeldust…He can make it."

"He's never been ridden, girl. You're crazy," argued Flynn.

"He'll let me."

"Take my saddle, then," he said.

"No, we'll go bareback with just his horsehair headstall. I'll tie the *mekate* back to itself under his chin for reins…He's run all of his life. Now, how do I get there?"

Flynn shook his head, picked up a stick and drew a map in the sandy bank of the creek. Lisanne nodded, turned and sprinted up the bank toward the area where the stock was picketed.

"Let's make a travois and head toward Jacksboro. It's almost twenty miles," said Fiona. looking down at the unconscious Bone. "Hope he can make it." She caressed the side of his face.

"He'll make it. Bone dies damn hard," added Loraine as she wiped the tears from her cheeks.

Flynn looked around. "Damnation, this is the same spot where my brother, Dixon, died two years ago."

§§§

CHAPTER TWENTY

JACK COUNTY, TEXAS

Lisanne leaned forward over Steeldust's neck, her long blond hair and his black mane flowed in the wind as he easily stretched out in his mile-eating gallop. The long-legged stallion could maintain this moderately paced gait of twenty-five miles an hour pace for more than an hour before slowing to a trot to rest and catch his breath.

"Run easy, boy, run easy. You can do this," she whispered in his ear.

They angled north of Jacksboro and south of Alvord in Wise County, toward the Wilson Ranch. The six hundred acre ranch was just the other side of the county line, southwest of the farming community of Rosston.

WILSON RANCH

Lucy sat bolt upright in her small bed in her room at Cletus and Mary Lou Wilson's new ranch. She jumped out of bed and padded barefoot in her nightgown into the kitchen where her adoptive mother, Mary Lou was fixing breakfast.

The smell of coffee, hot biscuits, bacon and pancakes filled the large kitchen.

"Good morning, Lucy, you're up early," said Flynn's sister.

"Something's wrong. Flynn and Fiona have been in a gunfight. Someone named Lisanne is coming to get me...Bone's been shot."

"Bone? Who's Bone?"

"Someone I will know in the future."

"Excuse me?...What are you talking about, honey?" Mary Lou frowned and shook her head.

"We have to go. They need me...Please."

Mary Lou's husband, Cletus, came through the back screen door from the barn with a three-quarters full galvanized pail of fresh milk.

"Who needs you?" he asked.

"Flynn, Fiona and Bone," Lucy replied.

"Bone?..."

"Don't ask," said Mary Lou as she put together several biscuits and bacon for her husband. "Here, eat these while you're hitching up the team to the buckboard."

"Uh, awright, where we goin'?"

Mary Lou looked at Lucy. He knew not to question Lucy's requests.

"West of Jacksboro...We must hurry," said the diminutive stranded alien, *Annuna*, masquerading as the Wilson's young daughter, Lucy.

Lucy's dog, Garrin, sitting at his food bowl, looked back and forth at Mary Lou, Cletus and his master.

Ken Farmer

JACK COUNTY, TEXAS

It took all three, Flynn, Fiona and Loraine to roll the two hundred and eighty-five pound Bone onto the ancient Indian transportation and lift the ends of the poles and attach them to the saddle.

They had ripped the bullet-riddled blankets into strips to make the travois, and then covered it with both Flynn and Loraine's ground tarps and blankets.

The travois was hitched to the seventeen hand chestnut part Friesian Bone had ridden. Flynn led the big horse behind Laddie as they headed back toward Jacksboro at a walk.

"Ya'll think you can find a little rougher road to take," said Bone weakly as the jostling aroused him from his unconscious state.

Loraine was riding on his right side while Fiona was on his left leading the pack horse.

"Well, how are you feeling, Bone?" asked Fiona.

"Like I been shot...Unnh," he groaned. "Any chance for a drink of water?"

Flynn reined to a stop while Loraine dismounted, unscrewed the lid, held her canteen to his mouth and let him drink.

"That's enough," she said after he had three swallows.

"Hell, Pard, got a hole in my lung, not my stomach," he said softly.

Fiona dismounted to check his wound. "Yes, and you're bleeding again."

She went back to one of the panniers on Potawatomi, got a clean towel, folded it up and handed it to Loraine. "Here, let's put a new compression pad on his wound. Wouldn't do to get him all the way to Jacksboro and have him bleed to death."

"Hey, I'm awake, you know," he grumbled.

"You're not going to be for long if you don't relax and keep quiet," said Loraine as she wiped the foamy blood from his mouth.

"You've just been waitin' for a time like this to get back at me, haven't you?"

"What? Me?" answered Loraine.

"What I thou…" Bone's voice faded as he passed out again.

"Can we go now? Still got fifteen miles to Jacksboro," said Flynn.

Loraine checked Bone's pulse and nodded. "Just as well…His pulse is a little erratic, but still strong. Let's go…I'm going to walk beside him."

Flynn nudged Laddie into an easy walk as Loraine led her horse and walked close to the travois.

WISE COUNTY

Lisanne bumped Steeldust back to a trot to allow him to rest and catch his breath. They were nearing the Wise and Cooke County line, still almost ten miles from the Wilson ranch.

Steeldust was only showing a little lather on his shoulders, but Lisanne didn't want to push the stallion.

"Easy, boy, I know you can run, but we got a ways to go."

He flicked his ears back at her as she talked softly to him and patted his neck.

Lisanne saw a wagon being pulled by two horses, also at a trot, in the distance as she topped a hill in the rolling grasslands.

The distance rapidly narrowed until she could make out a man, a woman, and a child in a buckboard.

She eased Steeldust to a walk, and then to a halt as they met the wagon. The horse blew out his nose and pawed the ground, irritated at stopping.

The man pulled back on the reins to the matched set of sorrel Morgans. "Whoa up there, boys, whoa," said Cletus Wilson.

The little girl with a pixie haircut and wearing a blue gingham dress stood up from her seat between the man and woman. A muscular yellow and white Amstaff Terrier sat in the back with his head cocked.

"Lisanne?"

"Oh, my goodness, you must be Lucy," replied the teenager. "How did you know me?"

"I'll explain later. I must get to Bone."

Lisanne looked at Cletus. "Mister Wilson, would you help Lucy up behind me?…We can go a lot faster than your team."

"I don't understand," he said.

He and Mary Lou looked at each other, both confused.

"Please, Father," said Lucy as she laid her hand on his shoulder.

"We have to, Cletus, Lucy knows what she's doing," commented Mary Lou.

"You're right...as usual." He stepped down to the ground, turned, lifted Lucy out of the wagon and set her on Steeldust, behind Lisanne.

"There's no saddle," he remarked.

"It doesn't matter, I will hold on to Lisanne...You stay in the wagon, Garrin. It's too far for you to run."

The pit bull whined and laid down, dejectedly, in the bed of the wagon with his head between his front paws. The faithful dog looked up at Lucy with his big brown eyes like he had been given a death sentence.

Lisanne turned Steeldust around in the road and squeezed him up into a lope back the way they had come.

"We'll follow you," shouted Mary Lou as they rode off.

STEELDUST

"I hope we can find them," said Lisanne. "There's no tellin' how far they've made it since I left at sunrise."

"Don't worry, I will tell you which way to go as we get closer."

Lisanne glanced back over her shoulder at the brown haired, four foot ten, Lucy. "You say so."

JACK COUNTY

"Bone's color doesn't look good," remarked Loraine. "Let's stop again."

Flynn reined Laddie up. "We need to keep goin'."

Loraine felt of Bone's forehead and cheek and frowned. "He's clammy."

She looked up at Fiona. "Get down and help me chafe his hands and arms. It'll help stimulate his blood flow...Mason, pull the travois over there at the side of the road under that big oak. Let's get out of the sun for a bit."

The marshal got down when Flynn stopped in the shade. She and Loraine each massaged a hand and arm vigorously.

"He doesn't look good, Loraine," said Fiona.

"I know," she said softly with concern showing on her face. "His pulse is getting weaker…How much farther, Mason?"

"'Bout five miles I make it…Another two and a half hours at the rate we're travelin'."

"Damn," muttered Loraine through clenched teeth.

Fiona looked up. "Please, Lord, help him. He's too good of a man to lose…Please," she asked as tears began to run down her cheeks.

They stopped the massage as Loraine checked his pulse.

"Oh, no," she exclaimed.

"What?" asked Fiona.

"I can't find a pulse…and he's not breathing…Please dear God, no, no," said Loraine as a large lump formed in her throat and she slumped to her knees beside the travois, her head dropped to her chest as sobs racked her body…

§§§

CHAPTER TWENTY-ONE

JACKSBORO, TEXAS

"I think you can get out of bed, now, if you want, Emma Lou," said Doctor Mosier.

"I'm all right, then?"

"Well, I don't want you to work at the restaurant for at least another twenty-four hours. Just take it easy…I'll see that Ruth Ann knows."

Ken Farmer

"Thank you. I'd like to sit with Gomer, if you don't mind?"

"No, be fine," he replied.

She got up from her bed, sat in a chair beside his bed, held his hand and squeezed it. Gomer looked lovingly at her and squeezed back.

"I love you," he said.

Emma Lou leaned over and kissed him softly on the lips. "I love you, too."

Mosier turned to Buster. "How're you feeling, son?"

"My side's sore as a risen, but better. Don't seem to be quite as weak, sir."

"Maybe you can have something a little more than broth. Say some chicken soup?"

"That sounds good."

"Just don't want you to eat anything that might make you strain, if you know what I mean." He smiled.

"Huh?...Oh, right." Buster blushed a little.

JACK COUNTY, TEXAS

"Look," exclaimed Flynn, pointing up the road.

Loraine's head jerked up from her chest to see Lisanne and Steeldust galloping over the top of the hill a hundred yards ahead. Dust rose in a column behind them.

"She's got Lucy with her," said Fiona as she noticed a small head sticking out from behind Lisanne with her short hair flying in the wind.

Steeldust slid to a stop at the edge of the shade near the travois. Lucy slid from the back of the stallion, dropped to the ground and ran over to Bone.

She felt of his head, and then his chest.

"It's too late, Lucy...It's too late," said Loraine through her tears.

The diminutive alien looked over at her. "Maybe not, Loraine."

"How do you know who I am?"

"Through Bone's mind. I saw his memories of us meeting in your time...He's an extra powerful sender, you know, and there's a reason." Her gaze shifted to Fiona. "You know what to do."

"Will this hurt my..."

"Not at all," Lucy replied as she crawled up on the travois beside Bone on his left side as Fiona laid down on his right. They joined arms over Bone's chest and, as if on cue, both became very still and closed their eyes.

A soft blue glow began to emanate from Lucy and Fiona's bodies and encompass Bone's.

"What's happenin'," asked Lisanne. "What's that blue light?"

"It's their life force," Flynn said softly without looking at Lisanne. "Lucy and Fiona saved my life a couple years ago this way when I was shot in the back...I had died, too. This may take a little while...Why don't you an' I take the horses down to that creek yonder an' water 'em?"

Lisanne nodded and stroked Steeldust's sweaty neck. "He's barely breathin' hard, but he does need water."

"That's an unbelievable horse," said Flynn.

"Told you...I need somethin' to rub him down with while we water him an' the others."

"I'll get a towel from the panniers...Let's undo the poles from Bone's horse so we can lay the travois flat on the ground...All the stock need water...And we'll need to fill the canteens."

Lisanne nodded again and glanced back down at Lucy and Fiona holding Bone as the glow got brighter and brighter. She could no longer make out their forms through the light.

"It's so bright." She shielded her eyes.

"Bone's a big man, it's taking a great deal of energy…Come on, let's go…Do you want to help, Loraine?"

She looked up at him and shook her head. "No, I have to stay here. He's my partner," her voice broke.

Flynn nodded. "I understand," he said as he loosened Laddie's cinch and picked up his reins along with Spot's and Loraine's.

Lisanne grabbed Steeldust's *mekate*, Bone's and Potawatomi's reins and followed Flynn down toward the creek. Newton and Barney padded along.

The blue aura around the three forms on the travois behind them intensified even more.

"The canteens are all nearly half full," Lisanne said as she hung them over her shoulder.

"They'll be really thirsty when they come out of the treatment Lucy is doin'…Trust me, been there."

Lisanne glanced at Flynn and frowned in confusion.

Down at the clear limestone-bottomed creek, Lisanne rubbed Steeldust dry with the towel as he drank.

The other horses and Fiona's mule were lined up along the bank, also drinking, along with Newton and Barney. Flynn was upstream ten yards, filling the canteens with the cool clear water.

When all the animals had drank their fill, Flynn and Lisanne led them back up the embankment to the large oak tree.

The blue glow appeared to be slowly fading and disappearing into Bone's body. Lucy and Fiona looked as if they were deep in slumber nestled next to the big man.

"His chest is moving!...He's breathing," exclaimed Loraine as she raised up on her knees.

Flynn gave the reins to the mounts he was leading to Lisanne to ground tie or picket while he walked over to the travois.

"He's alive. Thank God, he's alive," Loraine cried. "Thank you Sweet Jesus, thank you." She caressed the side of Bone's face and looked over at Flynn. "When will he wake up?"

"Not sure. When I woke up, Lucy and Fiona stayed out for a while as their bodies recuperated an' I drank a lot of water. I mean a lot...We just have to wait."

"Here comes the Wilsons," said Lisanne as she spied the buckboard topping the hill, the horses at a road trot.

In just a few minutes, the team drew up even with the tree. The dust cloud behind them blew on past with the slight wind.

"Whoa, boys, whoa up there," said Cletus as he pulled back on the reins.

Garrin jumped out of the back and ran over to sniff of Lucy's still form. He licked her arm and promptly laid down next to her as Newton and Barney trotted over to get acquainted.

"Is everything all right?" asked Mary Lou as she clambered down from the wagon.

"Well, so far," replied her brother. "We'll know in a bit...He had stopped breathin' like I did."

"This the same thing Lucy and Fiona did to you when you were shot?" she asked.

Flynn nodded. "Yeah, but he's a lot bigger than me...Think it's takin' longer."

Cletus started unhooking the team from the buckboard. "Gonna take the boys down to that creek and water 'em...They done good today."

"I'll help you, Mister Wilson."

"Thank you…Lisanne, isn't it?"

"Yessir." She smiled big as she took the lead to one of the geldings.

"I don't understand what Lucy's doin' at all," said Lisanne as they stood and watched the horses drink.

"To be honest, I don't quite understand it either," replied Cletus.

"Where's she from? I mean Mason told me ya'll adopted her."

He glanced over at her and grinned. "Well, that's the thing. See, she's not from around here…Lucy's from another world."

"What?"

Cletus nodded. "Her vehicle crashed an'…"

"That spaceship that crashed at Aurora a couple years ago? That was hers?"

"Yep. Hers an' her mate…He didn't survive. The town's folk gave him a Christian burial in the local cemetery. The article in the Dallas Morning News said he was not of this world…She hid out for a while, an' then pretended she was a abandoned mute child…Saw a dog get killed, that was Garrin, an' saved it like she's doin' Bone…"

"How did Mason an' Fiona find her?"

"Well, a cafe owner in Paradise was feedin' her an' the dog in his kitchen...Like I said, she pretended she was mute on account she couldn't speak our language then."

"This is amazin'...Just amazin'."

"Yeah, but that ain't all...When Mason and Fiona come into the restaurant to eat, he asked them if they could take her, bein' law officers an' all."

He bent down and filled the canteen he had brought. "Well, when they met her, she instantly could read both their minds...an' she let them read hers. Seems they're senders, too."

"That's how she knew about Bone?" asked Lisanne.

"Guess so. Part of this whole business I don't understand."

"But, she's just a child."

Cletus laughed. "Actually, hon, she's several thousand years old."

"What?" Lisanne was stunned and almost staggered.

"Somethin' 'bout the way her people, the Anunnaki they're called...her real name is Annuna, by the way...travel from their world to ours an' back…they don't age much. This is all way beyond what I can understand, you see."

"I do…Makin' my head spin," commented Lisanne. "'Specially don't understand how she's able to heal folks."

"You're not alone there…Just thank God she can…Ready to head back up?"

She nodded, turned and started walking back up the bank. "Now, need to find out where Bone an' Loraine are from…they're…they're, I don't know, so different…He wears his hair real short an' flat on top. They both have unusual guns, talk funny…just a bunch of things."

"Can't help you there. Haven't know 'em long as you," Cletus replied.

Bone groaned, flicked his eyelids, smacked his lips and looked around. "Dang, I'm thirsty," he said as Lisanne and Cletus got back from the creek and tethered the horses.

"See? What'd I tell you?" Flynn said to Lisanne as he unscrewed the cap to his canteen.

He knelt down, leaned over Fiona and held the canteen to Bone's lips.

STEELDUST

The big man drained almost half the canteen before he took a breath. "Damn, that's good. I was dry as a powder puff…What happened? Didn't I get shot?" He looked down at his chest at a red scar. Huh, it's gone…Gonna need a shirt."

Flynn nodded. "Yeah, Lucy an' Fiona did that healin' thing…and Fiona washed the blood out of your shirt, but it's got a hole in it…Looked like an undershirt with the sleeves cut off."

"Yeah, we call 'em T shirts." He tried to sit up. "Whoa, weak as a kitten. Might need some help here." He glanced to his left. "Hey, that's Lucy. Lot younger, but it's still Lucy… Where'd she come from?" Then he looked the other way. "What's wrong with her an' Fiona?"

"They're restin'," answered Flynn.

"From what?"

Flynn chuckled. "Tell you later." He stood at the wide end of the travois and held his hand out for Bone to grab.

"Will this wake 'em up?" he asked as he pulled himself to his feet and stepped over Fiona.

"Doubt it," replied Mason.

§§§

CHAPTER TWENTY-TWO

JACK COUNTY, TEXAS

The sun settled on the western horizon and sent silver edged red arrows across the blue sky to the east.

Bone and Loraine sat side-by-side on a log, sipping on cups of Arbuckle coffee, watching Fiona and Lucy, still on the travois, asleep.

Flynn walked up with his own cup. "A watched pot doesn't boil."

Bone looked up at the sheriff. "You saying that they aren't going to wake up long as we're watchin'?"

"Didn't say that…It's just an expression. Just know they won't wake up until their bodies have recouped an' are ready, is all."

"I heard my grandmother say once when I was just a little kid…Think she got it from her mother…'One Servant runs for fresh Water, another for Coals. The Bellows are plied with a will. I was very Hungry; it was so late; a watched pot is slow to boil, as Poor Richard, also known as Ben Franklin, said'," commented Bone.

"Huh…Sounds like somethin' my bride would say…Fact is, I think she has before. She loves to quote people and books."

"Noticed," said Bone as he took another sip of coffee.

"Looks like we're getting ready to spend the night here," commented Loraine.

"I'd say." Flynn glanced over at the campfire. "Sis is gettin' fixin's out for supper. Glad we brought plenty in Potawatomi's panniers."

Loraine started to get to her feet. "Guess I'd better go over and see if I can help."

"Wouldn't bother. She'll just run you off...won't even let Fiona help in the kitchen when we go visitin'."

"Know the feeling," she said as she settled back down and looked over at Lucy and Fiona again. "How long did they sleep after they worked that procedure, or whatever it's called, on you?"

"'Bout two hours, as I recall...'Course Bone's got me by around seventy-five pounds or so...May take a bit longer." He patted the big man's shoulder and grinned.

"Already been almost three," commented Bone as he looked at the black dive watch on his left wrist.

"I know...Interestin' way to carry a watch. Don't have to take it out of your pocket."

Bone looked at it again. "Yeah...Called a Dive Watch."

Flynn frowned. "What? Dive Watch?...What does that mean?"

"My pard here and my Padrino and I do a lot of SCUBA diving..."

"Awright, I'll bite, what's SCUBA divin'?"

"Self Contained Underwater Breathing Apparatus."

"Oh, like in that novel Jules Verne wrote back in 1870, *Twenty Thousand Leagues Under the Sea*."

"Yep, but that was fiction, we have the real deal in our time. Much more compact...We can swim around with a small tank of compressed air on our back and fins on our feet for up to an hour or so...Even got a new device called a rebreather that eliminates the tank."

"Huh...But, what do all those dials an' things do?"

"Oh, besides tell time and act as a stop watch, the date...The date thing doesn't work here. Guess it can't go backward..."

"Like you dancing," commented Loraine.

"Just had to get that in, didn't you?"

"Uh, huh."

"Humf...Wait'll I recoup."

"I'll be here," she said.

"Yeah...It also tells the wearer how deep underwater he is an' how long he can stay down...Lots of cool stuff. But, not near as cool as this bracelet." He held up his right arm.

"What does 'cool' mean?"

"Uh, neat…useful…"

"Handy?"

"Close enough."

"When Lucy showed me her bracelet, I asked how I could get one an' she said she didn't have the parts or tools to make one on our planet."

"She made this one special for me on board one of their giant motherships after she was rescued," added Bone.

Huh…Guess I'll have to wait awhile," commented Flynn.

"About 116 years, I make it." Bone caught a movement out of the corner of his eye. "Well slap Aunt Gussie in the face. Look who's wakin' up."

Lucy blinked several times and hugged Garrin when he crawled up on top of her and licked her face. "Thank you, sweet thing," she said and then looked over at Bone.

"How are you feeling, Bone?"

"A little weak and chest's a bit sore…Back is a little, too…Thank you, Lucy. Believe you saved my life."

"Had to. We have to meet in a hundred years or so, we have things to do…And about your back. The bullet is flattened against your shoulder blade.

You'll have to get a physician to remove it later…My healing ability doesn't include removing objects."

"How did you know about me?"

"I will tell you in the future that you're a powerful sender…A trait you inherited from more than one source. I knew when you were shot…I can read your thoughts and memories from a long way."

"Like my brother did when I was shot in the back an' died for a moment," said Flynn.

Lucy smiled and nodded. "Something like that."

Fiona began to stir. She raised her head and looked around.

Flynn handed a canteen to each of them. They eagerly took them, unscrewed the caps and drank for a long moment.

"You remembered," said Lucy.

"I did. Think I've drank two all by myself," said Flynn.

"How long were we asleep?" asked Fiona as she rubbed the back of her neck.

"Just about three hours," replied Bone. "Your sister-in-law is fixin' supper."

"Wonderful. I'm not only thirsty, but famished also."

"So am I," said Lucy as she got to her feet a little wobbly.

Bone reached out his hand to offer support. "I had to have help gettin' up."

"But, you were dead," said Loraine. "Of course you've been the same way when you've had too much beer."

"Your turn's comin', Pard."

"Like I said earlier...I'll be here." She grinned and elbowed his side.

An hour later everyone was sitting around the fire, having their evening coffee after a supper of son-of-a-gun stew prepared by Mary Lou.

Bone turned to Lucy. "Well, that's pretty much what has happened up to this point and guess you know why we were heading to see you."

"Yes, I do."

"I suppose we can talk about it, since everybody seems to be in the know..."

"Except me," interjected Lisanne. "I don't really know who you and Loraine are...I mean you've saved my bacon twice, but I know you're not from around here."

"That's putting it mildly," commented Loraine as she glanced at her partner.

"Uh...we're from the future, Lisanne," said Bone. "Have you ever read Twain's *A Connecticut Yankee in King Author's Court*?"

"Yes, actually I have."

"Well, there you go," said Bone.

She blinked and shook her head. "Wow...Well, if I can believe Lucy is from another world, guess I can believe ya'll are from the future."

Lucy smiled. "To quote your William Shakespeare in his play, *Hamlet*, 'There are more things in heaven and Earth, Horatio, than are dreamt of in your philosophy'. It is the height of human egotism to believe that you are the only intelligent life in the wide universe."

"But, why are ya'll here?"

"That's our question, too, Lisanne," said Loraine.

"Got no clue...Well, maybe a little one, but that's why we went lookin' for Lucy when we got here a few days ago," added Bone. "I will inherit the Wilson Ranch from her..."

Lucy smiled at Cletus and Mary Lou.

"...in our time. So we knew where to go."

"That's interestin'," said Cletus.

"I know from their memories that we meet..." Lucy tilted her head toward Bone and Loraine. "...in 2014 and they saved my life and allowed me to be rescued by my people...I firmly believe it was ordained on the Great Obelisk."

"The what?" asked Lisanne.

"The Great Obelisk."

"I don't understand."

"You can compare it to your Christian Bible, Jewish Torah, the Hindu Mahabharata, or maybe the Muslim Koran...which was mostly taken from the Torah and the Bible."

"You mean God's word," Lisanne said.

"We refer to *God* as the Holy Entity. But, it's the same...*Elohim, Yahweh, Jehovah, Jesus*, *Allah*, *Chí-hóo-wah, Brahma, Aten*, the Creator, Great Spirit...any number of names. The simple fact is, there is only one Almighty God...we just use the *Holy Entity*. The Anunnaki is a matriarchal society and we refer to the Holy Entity as 'Her'."

"That makes sense," said Fiona.

"The early humans referred to us...the Anunnaki...as gods or deities. It took us millennia to get them to understand that there was only one real creator...But, back to the point."

"Thank you," said Bone as he rubbed his temples. "Lucy always gives me a headache when she starts fillin' in the holes."

"I'm sorry, Bone. I know I've told you all this in your time and there's much the rest of you aren't really ready for."

"What we need to know is..." Bone glanced at Loraine. "...is what are we doin' here and can we get back?"

"The answer to that is...I don't know."

"Oh, boy," mumbled Bone.

"I only believe that the Great Entity caused you to be here. She has a purpose that may not be for us mere mortals to know. And I suspect that as far as getting back to your time...that also may not be for you to know...until it happens."

"Kinda what I figured," said Bone.

"You may have to do what I'm doing," added Lucy.

"That would be?" asked Bone.

"Blend in until it's time for you to know...I suspect that if you return to your time, it will be through the same or possibly a different portal." Lucy paused and sipped her coffee.

"It's hard for Bone to blend in anywhere," said Loraine.

"You got room to talk, Double D," he cracked back.

"Damn you, Bone, I'm going to kill you."

He grinned. "Been there, done that."

"What does Double D mean?" asked Mason.

"Well, in our time, the part of women's, uh…undergarments that, well, lift and support, uh…are sized as A, B, C, D…Double D…" Bone's gaze drifted down to Loraine's ample breasts.

Mason's eyes followed and he grinned. "Oh! I…"

"Watch what you say, mister," said Fiona as she swatted him behind his head.

Lucy smiled at their good-natured banter. "I shouldn't be here either, but, here I am until I'm rescued and you've let me know when that will be."

"I see…I think…Then you'll age normally while you're here?" inquired Lisanne.

"Yes," she replied. "The Lucy Bone and Loraine know is much older."

"But, you carry your age well," commented Loraine.

"Can you explain how we got here?" asked Bone.

Lucy smiled. "I'll try. Our scientists believe that space and time are synonymous. It's called the space/time continuum."

"Oh, boy, here we go," commented Bone. "Wished Padrino was here to translate."

"You asked…We know that we can fold space and travel through, what are called 'worm holes', that's how we can get to your planet in a matter of moments.

"Our world of Tyrin is in Orion's Arm on the other side of this galaxy…over three parsecs or around a hundred million light years away."

"What's a light year?" asked Lisanne.

"The distance light can travel in one year," interjected Fiona. "An example would be we can see the sun when it comes up, but it takes around eight minutes for the light to reach Earth…the speed of light is 186,000 miles per second."

"Oh, wow," said Lisanne as she shook her head. "Guess that's fast."

"I'd say," added Flynn.

"We travel through these 'worm holes' or folds in the fabric of space to get here and we believe time is the same. Those spiral petroglyphs around the world indicate where one of those folds or what our scientists refer to as a recurring electromagnetic vortex acts as a portal or gate to another time."

"How are they activated," asked Bone.

Cletus, Mary Lou, Lisanne and Flynn gazed at Lucy with blank looks on their faces.

"At this point in the space/time continuum...Even we don't know. Those that came before us who created the portals didn't leave any explanation of exactly how they worked."

"And that's the name of that tune," commented Bone.

"We just know that when someone travels to another time and then goes back...that they get there at the same time they left."

"Huh?" said Flynn.

"Oh, I get it," commented Bone.

Loraine glanced at him. "Wonders never cease."

"Okay, Pard. Guess you knew what Lucy was talkin' about all along."

She flashed her white teeth. "Pretty much."

"So, we're stuck here until we aren't, but if we get back, we won't really have left," said Bone.

Lucy smiled and nodded her head.

"If you can travel from your world to here in a matter of minutes, why will it take so long for your people to come for you?" asked Lisanne.

"Our ships travel through the worm hole, as I've mentioned, but the signal I have to send can only go by what is called sub or normal space at the speed of light...Therefore, since it's over a hundred light years it will take about that time for them to know where I am."

Fiona got to her feet. "I think I need to take a walk. That's a lot of information to process at one time...Walk with me, Honey." She held out her hand to Mason.

He got to his feet and they strolled off toward the creek, hand in hand.

They walked slowly along the bank listening to the soothing night sounds of the cicada, crickets, owls, frogs and the occasional fish slapping the water of the slow moving creek.

"Good gosh almighty, that was amazin', think I understood maybe half of what Lucy said," commented Flynn.

Fiona stopped, turned and put both arms around his neck and kissed him softly. "Well, see if you can understand this, Mason Flynn."

"What's that, Fiona Flynn?"

"You're going to be a father."

§§§

EPILOGUE

JACK COUNTY, TEXAS

The small caravan stopped two miles out of Jacksboro at the crossroads leading northeast to Rosston.

"We're goin' to head on back to the ranch, got chores to do," said Cletus.

"Ya'll come on up for a visit when you get done in Jacksboro," added Mary Lou.

"Need to check on Gomer, Emma Lou…"

"And Buster," interrupted Lisanne.

"Yep, and Buster…an' not countin' the reports my sweet bride an' I have to write up on the last two days," said Flynn.

"Also need to send the undertaker out with a couple of wagons to collect the bodies…What's left, that is. I'm sure the critters have already been at them," added Fiona. "We'll be up in a few days."

Lucy climbed over the seat to the back of the wagon and motioned to Bone and Loraine to ride closer.

"Lean over, Bone." She reached up and hugged his neck. "Now you, Loraine." Lucy hugged her, too. "I'm so glad we got to meet in this timeline."

"Me too," responded Loraine.

"And me, Lucy." Bone glanced at Fiona and Mason. "Make that double for me." He winked at her.

"I know…See you soon," she responded.

"Figured you did and count on it," replied Bone.

"Come up, boys," said Cletus as he flicked the ribbons over the horse's rumps and clucked at them.

STEELDUST

Lucy grabbed the back of the seat to keep from falling and waved good bye to the others as the wagon rolled down the dusty road.

They turned their mounts and headed toward Jacksboro at a collected trot.

Lisanne heard a loud whinny behind them, reined up and turned to see Steeldust atop a ridge, rearing and pawing the air. The others also stopped, turned and followed her gaze.

"What about Steeldust?" asked Flynn.

"I told him to go back to his herd." Lisanne looked over at the big man, and then back at Flynn. "He's the reason Lucy was able to save Bone…He covered over fifty miles in less than two hours."

"That's an amazing feat. That stallion is darn sure responsible for me still being alive an' breathin'," commented Bone as he stood in his stirrups, turned his body and saluted Steeldust.

"He deserves his freedom…But, he'll come when I need him…I'll still get his babies," Lisanne said with a grin. "He'll keep his ladies close to my ranch. I'll see that no one bothers them an put out a little extra feed for 'em."

"My pard an I got your back on that, Lisanne…Long as we're here," said Bone.

"You can count on Mason and me, too," added Fiona as the group trotted up to a big red board-and-batt barn that was Mom Tucker's Livery and pulled rein.

The fifty year old proprietress strolled out of the double wide front doors of the stable, removing her corncob pipe from her mouth.

"Well, ya'll weren't gone long as I expected."

"What, Mom? No faith in our abilities?" stated Flynn as he stepped down from Laddie.

"Not that, but ya'll were goin' after a whole passel of ne'er-do-wells an' yahoos...Figured they'd split up on you."

"They did," answered Fiona. "But, Bone and I went after the Sinclair bunch while Mason and Loraine took after Wild Bob and his gang...Didn't take long."

"They were way out of their league," added Bone.

Mom grinned and shook her head. "'Magine so...Rest of ya'll get down. Haircut an' me'll give your mounts special treatment an' unpack your panniers for you."

"Thanks, Mom, 'preciate that," answered Flynn.

STEELDUST

"Just water and check my mare's feet, Mom. I'm only in town long enough to see 'bout Buster over to Doc Mosier's," said Lisanne. "Then gotta head out to the ranch."

"Hear tell the boy's gonna be awright. Real lucky, he is...Real lucky," Mom replied.

"Thank the Lord," commented Lisanne.

"Let's head on down to Doctor Mosier's an' then go to Sewel's for some lunch," said Fiona.

"Now you're talking. Could eat the sideboards off a garbage wagon," added Bone.

"That all you think about...is eating," quipped Loraine.

"I been shot, Pard...Need my energy," replied Bone.

"You've been what?" asked Mom looking at the hole in his olive drab T shirt.

"Explain later," said Flynn as he led the group down the street toward the doctor's clinic leaving Mom with a puzzled expression.

"Gonna have to go by the haberdashers after we see the kids and feed our faces. Loraine and I need some duds. All we got is what we're wearing...Folks are staring at the hole in my shirt,"

261

commented Bone as they approached the door to the clinic.

"Not counting the fact we've been wearing these since we got here and they look funny compared to the natives," added Loraine. "Lucy said we need to blend in."

"Yeah, lots of luck on that. We don't have a haberdashers…You'll have to make do with Barber's Mercantile," said Flynn as they entered the front office. "Hey, Gertrude, how're the kiddos?"

She got up from her desk. "Sheriff! Glad to see ya'll are back in one piece."

He glanced at Bone. "Well, mostly…Can we see the patients?"

"Of course. They're awake and hungry."

"That's a good sign," Flynn replied as he led the way through the door into the hospital area.

"Sheriff! Marshal!" said Gomer as he raised up a little.

"How are you feeling, Gomer?" asked Fiona.

"Fair to middlin'…Fair to middlin'. Bit sore an' cain't breath through my nose yet with all that packin' the doc shoved up in there."

"Best way to keep it from moving around. I reset it with a couple of stainless steel rods while he was

STEELDUST

still out cold," said Mosier as he walked in from his office.

"Shore glad I was unconscious when he was doin' that. From the way he explained it, sounded like it would hurt like all get out," commented Gomer, glancing at the white-haired physician.

Lisanne took Buster's hand and held it. "How are you, Buster?"

He grinned and squeezed her hand. "Feel more like I do now than I did...If I can just keep from laughin' at Gomer."

"The good Lord was watching out for him when he got shot. The bullet went in at the edge of his stomach, spun around the inside of his ribcage and exited out the back right next to his spinea erector...Didn't even break any ribs," said the doctor.

"What's a 'spinea erector?" asked Gomer.

"Backstrap," replied Loraine.

"Oh!" He glanced over at Mosier. "Why didn't you just say so?"

"I did...And it's time for both of you to get up and walk around a bit. Don't want to have to treat you for pneumonia."

"I'll help Gomer," said Emma Lou.

Ken Farmer

"And I'll help Buster. Don't need either one fallin'," said Lisanne.

"That's good, thank you," said Mosier. "Don't go too far."

"We won't," she replied as they headed out the door.

"Say doc, I've got an...uh, old bullet wound that's, uh...starting to bother me some. Didn't go all the way through and is lodged against my shoulder blade. Think you can get it out?...Left side."

"Turn around and push your left shoulder forward."

Doctor Mosier palpated the area. "Well, it's at the edge of your scapula. I can feel it with my fingers...I can take it out now, if you wish."

"Gotta knock me out?" asked Bone.

"No, no. I'll use a local anesthetic some doctors are trying back east. It's injected subcutaneously."

Loraine raised her eyebrows.

"It's a powder solution I have to make up that will deaden the area so I can remove the offending item...Take your shirt off and lie down on that table over there."

"Whatever you say, Doc," Bone said as he did as requested.

He looked at the red scar on Bone's chest. "Doesn't look all that old."

"What can I say?"

"Well, hang your left arm off the table so your shoulder blade is pulled forward."

"Can do."

"Gertrude, if you'll wipe the area down with some iodine, I'll mix up the anesthetic."

"Yes, sir," she replied.

Mosier stepped over to a cabinet, took out a bottle of distilled water and a vial of white powder. He took a small chemical spatula, dipped out some of the powder and put it in a glass test tube. Adding some of the water, he shook it vigorously and held it up to check the solution.

He picked up a syringe, stuck the needle down into the tube and drew up ten milliliters. Mosier tapped the side of the glass syringe and pushed the plunger slightly, expelling any air trapped inside.

"Patient ready, Gertrude?"

"Yes, sir."

The doctor put on some of the new white thin rubber gloves being manufactured by Goodyear and found the bullet again. He injected three milliliters subcutaneously on three sides of the object and handed the syringe to Gertrude.

"Now we'll give that a minute or so…"

"Whooo, makin' my lips feel funny already, doc," said Bone. "Ha, my nose is numb."

"It does go into the blood stream pretty rapidly. May give you a slight feeling of intoxication," he said as he picked up his scalpel.

He put a finger on each side of the bullet to hold it in place and made a half-inch incision just through the skin.

"Hello!" Mosier exclaimed as the lead bullet literally popped out of the cut.

He picked it up with his thumb and forefinger from Bone's back. ".45 caliber, I'd say…You agree Sheriff?"

Flynn and Fiona both took a good look at the misshapen slug.

"Believe you're right, Doc…"

He was interrupted as Bone began to sing, "*Just take those old records off the shelf, I'll sit and listen to 'em by myself…Today's music ain't got the same soul, I like that old time rock 'n' roll.*" He got a silly grin on his face…

"He's drunk," said Fiona with a smile.

"Oh, wait until he gets wound up," added Loraine.

"What's rock 'n' roll?" asked Flynn.

"Music from where we come from," answered Loraine. "One of Bone's favorite songs by Bob Seger."

"*I go out walkin' after midnight, Out in the moonlight, Just like we used to do, I'm always walkin', After midnight, searchin' for you...*" Bone wailed, badly off key.

"He likes country and Patsy Cline, too," said Loraine.

"How long is he goin' to be that way?" Flynn asked Mosier.

"Shouldn't be long. The liver oxidizes it very rapidly...Plus I only gave him a very small amount."

"Wow, what was that stuff, doc?" Bone asked as he blinked his eyes a couple of times and stretched his face to relieve the rapidly subsiding numbness.

"It's an extract from the coca plant in South America...They call it cocaine," said Mosier.

"Oh, boy," said Bone.

Loraine rolled her eyes.

"See, I think it's wearing off already," said Mosier as he tied off the last stitch.

Gertrude wiped the closed incision with more iodine.

"We'll head on over to Sewel's and order lunch while you finish up with Bone," said Flynn with a chuckle. "The special for ya'll?"

"Good for me," answered Loraine

"Think I want a steak the size of a wash tub," said Bone. "Medium rare."

The Flynns were smiling as they closed the door to the clinic behind them and headed toward the restaurant, followed closely by Newton and Barney.

"Bone is hilarious," said Fiona. "Reminds me of you when you've had too much tequila."

"Haw," Flynn replied.

Doctor Mosier stepped into the front office as Bone sat up on the table, pulled his T-shirt back over his head, and then motioned for Loraine to lean over to him. "You realize, don't you, Pard..." He glanced at the door once more and whispered, "...Sheriff and Marshal Flynn are my great-grandparents?"

§§§§

PREVIEW
of the
Next Exciting
Historical Western Novel
from

KEN FARMER

CHAPTER ONE

PARIS, TEXAS

"When the Secretary of the Navy reaches the Seven Devil Hills up in the Kiamichi Mountains on his hunting trip, that's when you and your men move, got it?…Kill his entourage, kidnap the Secretary and take him to the hideout."

"Hear tell he's purty salty an' good with a gun, Boss," said Brewster.

BONE

"What of it? You got enough men…Don't care if that four-eyed, blue nose is old scratch himself. You know the plan…just take care of it."

The Boss opened a hand-carved walnut humidor, pulled out an expensive Cuban cigar, smelled the length of it, and then snipped the end off with his cutter. He picked up his new pistol-shaped silver lighter, warmed the the cigar, lit it and blew a cloud of blue aromatic smoke over his balding head.

The portly well-dressed man removed the cigar from his mouth, held it up and rolled it through his fingers, looking at the burning end.

"Teddy Roosevelt is going to make us a lot of money," the boss said as his rough-dressed gunman, Tarlton Brewster, opened the paneled mahogany door and left.

A nondescript young man in a gray three-piece suit and black bowler sat on a bench across the street. He held an open newspaper in his hands as if he were reading it, but was actually looking just over the top at Brewster as he left the two story brick building.

The slender gunman untied his horse tethered to a ring in an iron post set in the concrete sidewalk, mounted and rode down the red brick street north toward the edge of town.

The man in the bowler glanced down the street at a large black cowboy leaning against a lamp post in front of the Red River Saloon, rolling a smoke and nodded.

The cowboy pitched the unlit quirly to the street as he untied his dapple gray stallion from a hitchrail, mounted and followed Brewster out of town at a discrete distance.

The watcher in the suit folded the newspaper, stuck it under his arm, strolled down to the end of the block to the Western Union office and entered.

JACKSBORO, TEXAS
SHERIFF'S OFFICE

Sheriff Flynn put down the stub of a yellow #2 pencil he'd been writing on a tablet with. "Well, looks like the total reward on Wild Bob an' his gang comes to five thousand, five hundred dollars...You and Loraine will have some money to live on...before you go find a way to go back to your time...assumin' that you do."

BONE

"Is that on the first time or the second?" asked the giant of a man sitting on the corner of the sheriff's desk.

Flynn furrowed his brow and looked up. "Good question, Bone...does it matter?"

"Well, yeah. Need to share it with you and Fiona if it was the second."

"In my humble opinion, it would be the first, since they escaped while under my control."

"Still think we should share it with you...After all ya'll have another mouth to feed on the way." Loraine winked at Fiona.

"Now, sweet Loraine, we don't need it, but thank you for the consideration...We don't depend on our salaries as law enforcement officers to live off of...We've collected more than our share of rewards in the last few years...So there."

"I'd say let's go down to the bank an' I'll sign off on the disbursement of the bounties...You can open an account."

"Super! Then we can go to Barber's, buy some clothes, get some rooms at the hotel or boarding house and have a long hot bath," said Loraine. "Tired of trying to stay upwind from Bone."

"Need to take a whiff of yourself, D." He grinned, stuck up his massive hand and caught the cup the attractive, ample breasted, Hispanic woman threw at him.

"Damn you, Bone, one of these times you're going to miss."

"Not likely…Say, is there a laundry around we can send these things to?…Might need 'em."

"There's Sing Lu's just this side of Mom's Livery," said Fiona.

"Saw that. Maybe they can sew up that hole." Loraine stuck her finger in the bullet hole in his upper chest.

"Ow, that's still a bit tinder, Pard." He looked back at Mason. "What will the bank say about our social security numbers?" asked Bone.

"Your what?"

"Social…"

Loraine interrupted her partner. "Don't have social security until 1935, Bone."

"Oh, right, knew that…Probably a good thing."

"What's social security?" asked Fiona.

"It's a program instituted by the government that takes a percentage of what people make in their lifetime and then pay it back to them monthly when they reach age sixty-five. They call it the federal Old-Age, Survivors, and Disability Insurance program," replied Loraine.

"And the government administers it?" Fiona inquired.

"Uh, oh," commented Flynn.

"You got that right, Sheriff," said Bone nodding. "They can screw up an anvil."

"Well, not happenin' yet, so let's trundle down to the Cattlemen's Bank of Jacksboro an' take care of business…Shall we?"

"We're with you, Sheriff," replied Loraine. She took a last sip of her coffee and set the cup on Mason's desk.

The others got up and headed out the door followed by the red and white Border Collie, Newton. Bone and Loraine were a few feet behind Mason and Fiona.

Loraine leaned toward Bone and whispered, "Are you not going to tell them you're their great-grandson?"

"Still thinkin' on that. They got enough on their plate right now. Don't know that it'll serve any purpose…Maybe later."

She shook her head. "Your choice…They already know we're from the future."

He chuckled. "What would I call them…Grandma an' Grandpa?"

"Not unless you want to get shot," she replied with a grin.

"True."

Thirty minutes later, they walked out of the bank.

"Good thing you were with us, Mason. That banker was sure looking at us funny."

"Yeah…Well, least you got some walkin' around money, Bone," said Flynn. "An' smart to use the address of Cletus an' Mary Lou's ranch, too."

"Good idea puttin' five grand in the bank and keepin' two fifty each. Now let's go get some clothes. Hate to give up my BDUs…"

"What are BDUs?" Fiona interrupted Bone.

He pointed at their camo cargo pants. "These…Stands for Battle Dress Utilities. Can carry a lot of stuff in these big pockets on the side…There's eight pockets altogether and the trousers are made out of a what they call a rip-stop material."

BONE

"I like the fact that they blend in with woods an' foliage," added Flynn.

"Like wearing buckskins on the trail. I've got a full set...including knee-high Apache style moccasins," said Fiona.

"Love to have some," commented Loraine. "And a pair of those knee-high moccasins you mentioned."

"I can sent ya'll measurements to my grandmother up in the Nations just outside of Tahlequah...she's Cherokee. She and some of her friends can make you both a set in a week or so," offered Fiona.

"Cool," said Bone. "Got to thinkin'..."

"That's scary," quipped Loraine.

"Keep it up, Pard, just keep it up," Bone replied. She got a big grin across her face. "Plan to."

"Got to thinkin' that mercantile may not have much in my size." He glanced at some of the people on the street there in Jacksboro.

"Got a point there, Bone," said Flynn. "May have to go by a seamstress'. We got several in town. They can measure you and make whatever you want...Should be able to get jeans and a union suit, though...Need to get a hat, too."

"Damn, hate to lose my cap." He reset his department issue baseball type hat on his head.

"Makes you stick out like a sore thumb, Bone," said Loraine. "Not that you need a whole lot of help."

"Point," he replied.

Flynn opened the right side of the twin nine-foot tall half glass door for the others, ringing the two inch brass bell attached to the header. He followed them inside the fifty-foot wide mercantile.

"Huh, this is almost like a Walmart back home. Got everything from hardware, to guns an' ammo, to clothes and groceries," said Loraine.

"There's a better gun store down the street. They just carry guns and ammunition. The owner's a gunsmith, too," commented Fiona. "Can custom make a lot of stuff like holsters and specialty ammunition…He tuned up Mason's Peacemaker to be like mine."

"How's that?" asked Bone.

She took out her right hand .38-40, opened the gate and ejected the live rounds, closed it and spun the cylinder and held it up. "See how the hammer is flattened and flared to my thumb side?"

"Uh, huh," replied Loraine.

BONE

"It makes it much easier and a lot faster to just drag the side of my thumb across it to cock it as I draw. I can squeeze the trigger as soon as I clear the holster...Plus the trigger pull is a little less than two pounds."

"Holy cow...like a feather," exclaimed Bone. "May have him see what he can do for my 500...and see if he can make me some ammo along with a holster and gunbelt like ya'lls."

"Doubt he can do much for my Kimber 1911 Stainless Classic II...Got a seven round magazine plus one in the chamber."

"Double action, isn't it?" asked Fiona.

"Yes...Trigger pull is about 4.5 pounds. May see if he can soften that up a little...Kinda used to it, though," Loraine replied.

"Like to try it sometime."

"Me too," said Mason.

"Like to try your's too," Loraine said.

"We should go out behind the office later an' do some target practice," offered the sheriff.

"That'll work...Need to check on some .50 cal ammo first, though," said Bone.

"We'll go by Newly's Gun Shop after lunch."

"Sounds like fun," commented Loraine as she started going through some clothes Fiona had directed her to.

"The dresses are over against that wall," said Fiona as she pointed.

Loraine looked askance at the tall marshal. "Uh, I rarely find occasion to wear a dress, Fiona. Not much call for it in my line of work...unless I go undercover."

Fiona grinned. "My sentiments exactly."

Bone glanced over at the two very attractive women. "Ya'll make a pair, you know...Loraine's 5'3" and you're what, Fiona, about 5'11"?"

She grinned. "An even six feet in my stockings. Got my height from my Italian grandfather. He was about your height."

"You don't say? What a coincidence," said Bone with a smile.

"You and Loraine make quite a partnership too...6'8" and 5'3"," added Mason.

"Yeah, she hides under my arm like a duckling when it rains."

"Damn you, Bone, gonna kill you one of these days."

"You're too late, Pard, already been killed once," he countered, grinning.

"Well, it didn't take," she said as she picked up some black canvas riding pants with leather inserts in the seat and down the inside of the leg like the ones Fiona wore. "Have to have the legs trimmed off these some."

"Yeah, Loraine had to sue the city back home."

"Really? What for?" asked Fiona.

"She said they built the sidewalks too close to her butt."

"Damn you, Bone." Loraine looked around for something to throw.

"Hey, how about this?" He held up a dark green John Bull hat and put it on. "Wow, fits too."

"Looks like the one Clint Eastwood wore in *Pale Rider*," said Loraine.

"Who?" asked Flynn.

"Clint Eastwood...he's a big movie star in our time," said Bone.

"Movie star?" asked Fiona. "Oh, like that moving picture thing Edison invented he called a Kinetograph back in 1890."

"Sort of. In our time they make two to four hour full-length dramas...like plays. You go in a dark theater and watch them on a big silver screen. They're fun...Cowboys and Indians, cops and robbers, war films, love stories, musicals...you name it," said Loraine.

"Right...Bat Masterson filmed a fight between Gentleman Jim Corbet and John L. Sullivan last year in Garden City, Kansas...Got to watch the fight," commented Fiona.

"You worked with Bat Masterson?" asked Loraine.

"Sure. Bass Reeves, too. As you know, Bone."

"Love to work with him. He's a real lawman, exclaimed Bone. "They erected a larger than life-size bronze statue of him on his horse Flash in 2014 in front of the new US Marshals Service museum they're building in Fort Smith, Arkansas...The Marshals Service consider Bass to be the greatest marshal in their history." He glanced at Fiona and smiled. "Present company accepted, of course."

"Oh, goodness no. I'm not even in Bass Reeves' category. I felt like Jane in *McGuffey' First Eclectic Reader* when I worked with him...He's amazing."

"Don't let her fun you. She's been called the female Bass Reeves…and she doesn't backwater to any man," said Mason.

"Oh, you hush," she replied.

A young man with a flat-topped Western Union cap entered, ringing the bell again, and glanced around until he spotted Fiona. He approached and removed his hat. "Marshal Flynn?"

She turned. "Yes?"

He handed her a yellow envelope. "Telegram from Washington."

"Thank you." She opened it with her fingernail, extracted the flimsy and read it.

"Will there be an answer, Marshal?" the freckled-faced teenager asked, taking out a note pad and a stub of a pencil.

She nodded. "Will comply…Stop…Leave for Paris day after tomorrow…Stop…Board train in Gainesville…Stop…Special Deputy US Marshal F.M. Flynn…End." She handed the young man a Morgan silver dollar.

"Wow! Thank you, Ma'am."

"You're welcome…and don't ever call me, 'Ma'am'."

"Yes…Uh, Marshal." He nodded to her, put his cap back on and headed quickly to the door.

When he had left, she looked first at her husband, and then turned to Bone and Loraine. She held up the telegram.

"From the US Marshals Service head office through the Secret Service…That's interesting…Looks like ya'll are going to get to meet the legendary Bass Reeves after all." She grinned big.

"You're not goin', Missus Flynn," commented Mason.

Her steel-gray eyes snapped to her husband. "Oh, really? And pray tell why not?"

"You're pregnant."

"Oh, fiddlesticks, I'm barely two months along…I'll be the one to decide when I back off, Mason Flynn." She gave him that look of hers that would melt steel.

"See, that look? What did I tell you?" he replied.

§§§

I hope you enjoyed STEELDUST and the preview of the next novel in the series...BONE. It's always appreciated if you liked the read to leave a favorable review on Amazon and Good Reads.
Thank you,
Ken Farmer

Drop me a note any time. My email is:
pagact@yahoo.com

My Facebook page is:
www.facebook.com/KenFarmerAuthor

My author page on Amazon is:
www.amazon.com/default/e/B0057OT3YI

TIMBER CREEK PRESS

OTHER NOVELS FROM
TIMBER CREEK PRESS
www.timbercreekpress.net

MILITARY ACTION/TECHNO

BLACK EAGLE FORCE: Eye of the Storm (Book #1)
by Buck Stienke and Ken Farmer

BLACK EAGLE FORCE: Sacred Mountain (Book #2) by Buck Stienke and Ken Farmer

RETURN of the STARFIGHTER (Book #3)
by Buck Stienke and Ken Farmer

BLACK EAGLE FORCE: BLOOD IVORY (Book #4)
by Buck Stienke and Ken Farmer with Doran Ingrham

BLACK EAGLE FORCE: FOURTH REICH (Book #5) by Buck Stienke and Ken Farmer

AURORA: INVASION (Book #6 in the BEF) by Ken Farmer & Buck Stienke

BLACK EAGLE FORCE: ISIS (Book #7) by Buck Stienke and Ken Farmer

BLOOD BROTHERS - Doran Ingrham, Buck Stienke and Ken Farmer

DARK SECRET - Doran Ingrham

NICARAGUAN HELL - Doran Ingrham

BLACKSTAR BOMBER by T.C. Miller

BLACKSTAR BAY by T.C. Miller
BLACKSTAR MOUNTAIN by T.C. Miller

HISTORICAL FICTION WESTERN
THE NATIONS by Ken Farmer and Buck Stienke
HAUNTED FALLS by Ken Farmer and Buck Stienke
HELL HOLE by Ken Farmer
ACROSS the RED by Ken Farmer and Buck Stienke
BASS and the LADY by Ken Farmer and Buck Stienke
DEVIL'S CANYON by Buck Stienke
LADY LAW by Ken Farmer
BLUE WATER WOMAN by Ken Farmer
FLYNN by Ken Farmer
AURALI RED by Ken Farmer
COLDIRON by Ken Farmer
STEELDUST by Ken Farmer

SY/FY
LEGEND of AURORA by Ken Farmer & Buck Stienke
AURORA: INVASION (Book #6 in the BEF) by Ken Farmer & Buck Stienke

HISTORICAL FICTION ROMANCE
THE TEMPLAR TRILOGY
MYSTERIOUS TEMPLAR by Adriana Girolami
THE CRIMSON AMULET by Adriana Girolami
TEMPLAR'S REDEMPTION by Adriana Girolami

Coming Soon

HISTORICAL FICTION WESTERN
NO TIME to DIE by Buck Stienke (sequel to
Devil's Canyon by Buck Stienke
BONE by Ken Farmer

HISTORICAL FICTION ROMANCE
DAUGHTER of HADES by Adriana Girolami

MILITARY ACTION/TECHNO
BLACKSTAR RANCH by T.C. Miller

SY/FY
ANTAREAN DILEMMA by T.C. Miller

Thanks for reading *STEELDUST*. If you enjoyed it, I would really appreciate a review on Amazon. My Author Page is:

www.amazon.com/Ken-Farmer/e/B0057OT3YI

Email - pagact@yahoo.com

Personally autographed books available at my web site:

Web page: www.KenFarmer-Author.net

TIMBER CREEK PRESS

32137576R00174

Printed in Great Britain
by Amazon